"PLEASE DON'T DO THIS TO ME," SHE SAID.

"Don't do what? Don't care about you? Don't feel? Don't want you? Don't make it clear that there's a fire inside me because of you? Don't do what, Geneva?"

"Don't invade my life and turn it upside down on some kind of a lark. I wouldn't survive it if you did that to me."

"You know in your heart that that isn't my intention."

She felt herself weakening, felt herself giving in. She prayed that he'd just spoken the truth, because much more than her heart was at stake. Lives could be jeopardized if she made an error in judgment.

"I want to believe you," she admitted.

"You can, but I guess I'll have to keep proving it to you, won't I?"

"That may not be possible."

"I'll make it possible," he vowed.

WHAT ARE *LOVESWEPT* ROMANCES?

They are stories of true romance and touching emotion. We believe those two very important ingredients are constants in our highly sensual and very believable stories in the LOVESWEPT line. Our goal is to give you, the reader, stories of consistently high quality that may sometimes make you laugh, sometimes make you cry, but are always fresh and creative and contain many delightful surprises within their pages.

Most romance fans read an enormous number of books. Those they truly love, they keep. Others may be traded with friends and soon forgotten. We hope that each LOVESWEPT romance will be a treasure—a "keeper." We will always try to publish

LOVE STORIES YOU'LL NEVER FORGET BY AUTHORS YOU'LL ALWAYS REMEMBER

The Editors

FALLEN ANGEL

LAURA
TAYLOR

BANTAM BOOKS
NEW YORK · TORONTO · LONDON · SYDNEY · AUCKLAND

FALLEN ANGEL

A Bantam Book / August 1996

ISBN 0-553-44526-X

Published simultaneously in the United States and Canada

Bantam Books are published by Bantam Books, a division of Bantam Doubleday Dell Publishing Group, Inc. Its trademark, consisting of the words "Bantam Books" and the portrayal of a rooster, is Registered in U.S. Patent and Trademark Office and in other countries. Marca Registrada. Bantam Books, 1540 Broadway, New York, New York 10036.

PRINTED IN THE UNITED STATES OF AMERICA

OPM   0 9 8 7 6 5 4 3 2 1

My sincere thanks to
Earl H. "Trip" Maas III,
Attorney at Law,
San Diego, California.

I would like to acknowledge the
John Tracey Clinic in Los Angeles,
which is dedicated to the needs
of the hearing impaired.

ONE

Thomas Coltrane made his way down the back staircase of the converted Victorian-style mansion, his thoughts on the office space he'd just inspected and the two-year lease he'd subsequently signed with the property manager.

The three-room suite in what passed for an office building in Cedar Grove was a far cry from the entire top floor his former law firm occupied in an upscale San Diego high-rise. That fact relieved him. He had finally extricated himself from the trappings and aggravation of life as a litigator and, he'd managed to orchestrate his return to northern Nevada with zero fanfare.

Thomas felt the peace of mind of a man who'd made the right decision for the right reasons. He intended to keep practicing law, but this time defending individuals instead of multimillion-dollar corporate entities. It was the reason he'd followed in his late father's footsteps, gone to Harvard Law, and become an attorney in the first place.

After the hefty retainers and all the hassles that went with a high-profile career, he wanted a simpler life, a real life, the kind of life that had horrified his former partners when he announced months earlier his plans to leave.

In truth, he recognized how jaded he'd become in recent years, but he was working to erase the cynicism that had become a part of his personality. He had all the money he would ever need, and his reputation as one of the top five litigators in the country remained intact. Thomas knew that he possessed the ruthless, go-for-the-jugular instincts of a legal predator, just as he knew he needed to temper those instincts, and several others, if he intended to attract clients to his new law practice.

At least he no longer minded looking at his face in the mirror each morning when he shaved. That, he assured himself, was a major step in the right direction.

Thomas was strolling along a deserted ground-level hallway when he heard someone speak.

"Did you understand me?" A man, his tone intense.

Thomas deliberately slowed his footsteps.

"Yes, but I'm having trouble believing you," confessed a woman.

Her voice, a low breathless sound replete with shock, prompted Thomas to peer around the corner, wondering who and what he'd interrupted.

"I wouldn't lie about something this important," said the man who towered over the petite woman. She stood with her back to Thomas.

"You don't lie. You never have," she replied, her hands moving gracefully as she spoke. "He's really dead?"

Thomas recognized the way in which she used her hands. Sign language. He'd rarely needed to communicate in sign language since his mother died ten years earlier. The word *dead* belatedly registered in his head. Dead? He frowned.

"He's quite dead." The man also used his hands with a dexterity that indicated a long-term knowledge of signing. "My sources are reliable."

Thomas took a step forward, deciding to alert the couple to his presence, but he paused once more. An instinct he couldn't label urged him not to reveal himself just yet.

"I know your sources are impeccable," the woman said. "You give new meaning to the word *meticulous*. It's just that I can't quite take it all in."

"What's left of Jamal is in the ground."

"What's left? I don't understand."

"It's not important. The bottom line is that he can't harm you. He's been neutralized, and his followers have gone to ground. Everything associated with the man died with him, so there's no need to let his quest for vengeance haunt you any longer."

Neutralized. Interesting word, Thomas reflected.

She shook her head, her mane of hair shifting across her shoulders and down her back like a golden waterfall. "When? How?"

"Lebanon. A car bomb. The Mossad confirmed his identity."

Thomas blinked in surprise at the reference to the Israeli intelligence agency. Who were these people? he wondered.

"They're very capable," she conceded.

She has a gift for understatement, Thomas thought wryly. The Mossad was reputed to be the best intelligence-gathering service in the world.

"Quite capable," the man concurred dryly.

"It's been twelve very long years, Nicholas. I—" Her words abruptly ceased. She lowered her hands to her sides.

She's upset, Thomas realized. He watched

the man called Nicholas draw her into his arms and embrace her.

Thomas didn't move.

The man released her and stepped back a few moments later. "It's over, little one. Now you can finally relax and have a real life, the kind of life you've always wanted."

She tilted her head, peering up at him for a long moment. "Can I? I wonder."

"Don't wonder. Just do it."

"Old habits are hard to shake. We both know that."

Thomas heard the wistfulness in her voice.

The man smiled. "Have some faith in yourself. Hannah rehabilitated me, didn't she?"

"Hannah's not like most people. She wanted to understand, and she's never felt compelled to sit in judgment. She simply loves with some instinct that defies logic. Most people aren't quite so trusting or tolerant."

"Cynicism doesn't suit you."

"I'm just careful," she insisted.

"You're more than careful, and we both know why. It's time to find out if someone is capable of accepting you for yourself, don't you think?"

"I am accepted."

"Only by people you've allowed into your world. And they're too damn few. You need and deserve more."

"You're becoming as stubborn as one of those legendary mules from Hannah's home state."

He chuckled, his humor doing little to ease the harsh angles of his face. "Probably."

Shuddering, she pressed her fingertips to her temples.

Delayed reaction, Thomas thought. He'd seen the response to stress countless times, both in and out of courtroom. Yet he sensed that her reaction went far beyond simple stress.

Nicholas placed his fingertips beneath her chin, nudging her face so that she could see his lips as he spoke. "Start living. It's time. Hell! It's past time. You're thirty-seven years old."

She laughed, the sound both shaky and faintly erotic to Thomas's ears.

"I feel seventy-five right now. I guess I never expected the situation to end. Not in my heart, anyway."

"Patrick wouldn't have wanted you to live this way."

"Patrick meant well, but he—"

"But, nothing."

"Nicholas, do you think he ever understood what he set in motion? I tell myself he didn't, but sometimes . . . sometimes I still wonder."

Thomas saw the man's face turn to stone.

"Of course not. Otherwise, he wouldn't have done what he did."

Was Patrick her lover or husband? Thomas wondered as he watched the woman.

She squared her shoulders, then shifted her body. Thomas caught a glimpse of her profile. The stubborn tilt of her chin reminded him of a model from Dublin he'd once known. The delicate sculpting of her cheekbone hinted at an ethereal kind of beauty.

"I think he would have been better off with a son," she remarked.

"Gender wasn't an issue with him. He adored you, and you can't ever forget that."

Patrick must have been her father, Thomas concluded.

"I'm not sure what to do now," she admitted.

"Live your life and be yourself. You've always been a gift to those who love you. It's time to love yourself, and it's way past time to let the right man into your life."

Thomas waited for her response. The air in his lungs started to burn as he held his breath.

"I don't know if I can," she finally said. "I hate admitting it, but I'm afraid to trust anyone too much."

"Cowardice doesn't suit you."

Thomas disliked the hard edge in the

man's voice, but the woman didn't seem to mind. They've known each other for years, he realized.

"Thank you," she said in that low voice of hers. "Thank you for everything."

Everything? Thomas couldn't curb his curiosity. What did *everything* mean exactly? Had they been lovers? Were they lovers now?

"You've done so much for me," she said. "How do I even begin to repay you?"

"There's no need, Geneva."

Geneva. Not a run-of-the-mill name, but Thomas had already guessed that she wasn't a run-of-the-mill kind of woman. Not by any stretch of the imagination.

"Without you, Sean would be dead," he said. "Because of you, Hannah has her brother back, I can converse with my best friend again, and he has a life he's proud of. In the final analysis, I owe you."

"We're an unconventional family."

Nicholas leaned down, gathered her close, and pressed a kiss to her forehead. "You'd better get inside. The tourists are here en masse, and this is your peak season. I'll see you soon."

Nicholas grazed her cheek with his fingertips.

Thomas stiffened at the familiarity of the parting gesture. Pure reflex, he realized a heartbeat later, although he didn't understand his response. It was neither rational nor typical of his nature to feel resentment because he wasn't the one offering comfort to a woman he didn't know. He blamed his reaction on the thin mountain air of northern Nevada, then felt like a complete fool.

"I love you, Nicholas," she signed. "I wouldn't have survived if you hadn't—"

Nicholas interrupted her. "I love you, too, but you would have survived. You're a woman of many talents. Anyone who has ever known you realizes that."

Thomas once again debated the wisdom of revealing himself. In the end, though, he still hesitated.

The woman named Geneva exhaled shakily as she watched Nicholas make his way down the hallway that led to the rear parking lot. She then walked the final few steps to a door marked Private. Sagging against the door, she bowed her head and pressed fingertips to her temples.

When she straightened and glanced down the hallway, Thomas saw her face for the first time. The face of an angel. His gaze dipped, and he took in the contours of her body, which was precisely defined by the fitted jumpsuit she wore. An angel with the body of a centerfold.

He felt his insides tighten with sudden tension. His heartbeat picked up speed, his response to her physical attributes utterly primal, profoundly male.

She swayed suddenly, and he watched as she steadied herself by placing a hand against the doorframe. Genuine concern leaped to life within him, but he felt reluctant to rob her of her privacy at such a vulnerable moment by making his presence known.

Oblivious to her audience of one, she let tears spill from her eyes to trace damp paths down her cheeks and into the corners of her mouth. She cursed very softly.

Thomas heard the sound. No stranger to disappointment, he grasped the blend of frustration, shock, and defeat in her curse. He realized that he wanted to touch her, to comfort her. Gently. Tenderly.

What would it be like to feel her warmth and softness? He suddenly wanted to breathe in the fragrance of her skin and hair. And he wanted a taste of her.

Stunned, Thomas Coltrane didn't move for a long moment. This woman whose last name he didn't know, this woman who was a stranger touched a chord in him in an achingly familiar way that utterly baffled him.

Geneva reached into her shoulder bag with one hand and dried her cheeks with the other.

Thomas moved out of the shadows and approached her. He momentarily forgot that she might not hear him when he said, "Miss?"

She didn't answer. He spoke a second time, then realized that it was *her* ability to hear, not Nicholas's, that was impaired. She employed sign language out of necessity. Her voice, in particular the absence of tinniness, prompted him to conclude that, like his mother, she'd been a part of the hearing world before losing one of the key senses that most people take for granted. He reached out to her, but knew the second he touched her shoulder that he'd made a serious error.

As Geneva rummaged through the contents of her leather shoulder bag, her emotions swirled in turmoil, her thoughts were jumbled, and her mind was filled with images from the past.

Images of joy and sadness. Of destruction. Of people and places she would never see again. Images normally never recalled and that had consequently faded over time. They weren't faded now, however. They played vividly through her mind like a home movie.

When a hand settled on her shoulder, Geneva's survival instincts kicked in, instincts honed in her early twenties during a brief career as an explosives expert for hire. She jerked free, raised her arm in a smooth arc as she turned and knocked aside the hand. She simultaneously released her shoulder bag. It crashed to the floor.

"Time out!" the man shouted. "I didn't mean to startle you."

She stared at him with skepticism.

"I apologize," he said.

"Don't touch me." She spoke slowly, not bothering to sign the command. "Not ever."

He nodded.

"Move away from me. Now," she ordered.

Stepping back and keeping his hands palms up and open, he said, "You're safe. I wouldn't ever hurt you."

Not taking her eyes from him, Geneva bent at the knees and picked up her purse. She found her key chain as she straightened, slung the leather bag over her shoulder, and quickly inserted the correct key into the lock. Shoving open the door, she slipped inside without a backward glance.

Thomas stood in the hallway long after she slammed the door in his face. He wondered about Jamal. He wondered why she was so stunned by the news of his demise. He also wondered why she lived what sounded like a solitary life.

What kind of woman was she?

Have you lost your mind? a voice in his head promptly inquired. And have you forgotten that you're trying to simplify your own life?

He *had* forgotten, he realized as he walked out of the building and climbed into his car. Driving down the ice-encrusted streets of Cedar Grove to his hotel, Thomas Coltrane couldn't stop thinking about the woman called Geneva.

She intrigued him to a degree that no other woman ever had.

TWO

Although Geneva Talmadge had been accosted by strangers more than once in her life, that fact provided very little consolation to her rattled emotions. Once she secured the deadbolt lock on her office door, deposited her purse on her desk, and then sank into the nearest chair, she struggled to reclaim her composure. She had always made sure the world never saw her as anything other than a totally poised woman.

Geneva told herself that she could have moved past the startling encounter with ease had it not come on the heels of learning that the contract on her life, which had been in force for nearly twelve years, was no longer viable. She still found it difficult to believe that the threat was over and that the malevolent creature known as Jamal was dead.

Other than the few close friends whom she trusted with her life, neither the residents of Cedar Grove nor the seasonal visitors to the surrounding ski resorts knew anything about her past. People speculated, of course. Geneva suspected that they always would.

She'd long ago resigned herself to that particular fact. So had the other men and women who lived within the protective confines of the extensive acreage owned by ex-mercenary-turned-bestselling author Nicholas Benteen. Friend and mentor, he vigilantly shepherded his flock of retired warriors. Geneva knew he would until he drew his last breath.

She sighed, the sound ragged in the early morning silence of her Talmadge, Inc. office. Her pulse rate slowed to normal and her hands finally stopped shaking.

Geneva knew she wasn't paranoid, just cautious. Despite being urged by Nicholas to embrace a future that included a relationship with a man, she wondered how one discarded years of self-protective behavior.

It didn't really matter that the life she'd once lived had been nothing more than an accident of fate. Nor did it matter that the missions she'd been a part of had been sanctioned by a clandestine arm of the U.S. government.

She felt certain that what would really matter was a man's reaction to her life. A sane man would reject her. After all, how many mates could be expected to deal with the reality that the woman in their life had once been an explosives expert, and had spent a childhood as companion to a soldier-of-fortune father known for his bombmaking skills? Few, if any. Damn few!

Geneva recalled the tumultuous days of her youth following her mother's funeral. Her father had appeared out of nowhere, like a modern-day Pied Piper.

While most young girls her age attended high school, she traveled the world, experiencing diverse cultures and customs. As her peers gossiped about boys and shopped for prom dresses, she saw loyalty tested and lives sacrificed. She learned all her lessons at her father's knee, from several languages to the art of constructing a bomb.

Patrick's friends, who became her friends, and her protectors whenever a crisis occurred, had been an eclectic assembly—men and women who took life-threatening risks on a daily basis. They challenged fate and lived on the edge—of society, of acceptable behavior, of conventional perceptions of right and wrong—but always within the framework of a rigid code of conduct.

Regardless of the world's disdain for them, Geneva thought of these men and women as her family. They'd comforted her when Patrick succumbed to a heart attack in Algiers on her nineteenth birthday. Nicholas had assumed the role of older brother, taking her under his wing and granting her membership in his band of highly paid soldiers.

A few years later those same men and women carried her damaged body to safety when an explosive device malfunctioned during the final days of a civil war in Africa. They guarded her during a lengthy recuperation while her broken bones and shattered spirit mended. Allies in friendship, they all learned sign language—some even going so far as to supplement their skills with finger spelling— as a means of facilitating her ability to adapt to a seventy-five percent hearing loss.

When the time to retire finally arrived, they did so as a group in a carefully orchestrated manner. The former warriors struggled with the adjustment required of them as they settled into new lives and identities in northern Nevada, but they struggled together, their loyalty to one another, and in particular to Nicholas Benteen, absolute.

Geneva knew now what she'd always known. She couldn't change the past, even though she desperately wanted to. Neither could she conceal it and still maintain her integrity if she welcomed a man into her heart and life. The truth wasn't a negotiable commodity. It never had been, and she realized that it never would be if she hoped to sustain her self-respect.

Geneva surged up from her chair and made her way to the stockroom adjacent to her office. Donning a smock, she forced herself to calm down by doing a simple chore: restocking the display shelves of her specialty shop with jars of homemade jams and preserves. The task also reminded her that she'd come a long way from the Third World–country battlefields she once walked.

As was her habit, Geneva greeted each person who walked into her store that day with a welcoming smile. The melancholy she felt remained concealed from everyone. The only one who sensed it was her reclusive business partner, Sean Cassidy, Nicholas's brother-in-law. He didn't press her, though, because he already carried his own burdens from their shared past.

More memories, more thoughts about the past kept Geneva awake that night. That and the face of the man who had so thoroughly frightened her. Geneva abandoned her bed well before dawn. She showered and dressed, then drove twenty miles in the dark to her office. She dealt with invoices and mail order forms as she sipped coffee and indulged her appetite with one of Sean's newer creations—wild raspberry muffins.

She noticed the blinking light on the electronic panel atop her desk a few hours later. Wired to a state-of-the-art motion sensor, the red light alerted her to the presence of customers. Nicholas, ever vigilant about her security, had installed the device prior to the grand opening of the shop.

Glad for the distraction, she set aside the various documents she'd received from her business attorney and got up from her desk. Geneva glanced at her watch and smiled. She expected to find her only employee, Rose Treadwell, arriving for her first day back to work following a four-week vacation in the Middle East.

Geneva stumbled to a stop in her office doorway when she spotted the tall, dark-haired man with Rose—the man who'd startled her in a shadow-filled hallway. Shocked to see him again, she moved out of their line of sight and watched Rose, a sixty-five-year-old widow and lifelong Cedar Grove resident, embrace the man.

Shifting her gaze to their faces, Geneva concentrated on their expressions and the movement of their lips as they communicated.

"It's about time you paid me a visit, young man," chastised Rose.

The man grinned. "This isn't a visit, Aunt

Rose. I've leased an office, and I'm looking for a place to live."

"Oh, Thomas, you're finally coming home!" she exclaimed before hugging him once again.

"I am home. For good," he clarified once he released her.

Geneva paled, embarrassment flooding her even though there was no way she could have known his identity. He intended to live here? She groaned silently, then recalled Rose's comments about her nephew, the famous attorney and the somewhat infamous ladies' man. She fully grasped his seductive appeal, although it unsettled her to admit it to herself.

Geneva watched closely as his gaze wandered through the spacious interior of her shop. She saw the appreciation in his expression as he took in the display shelves laden with a wide selection of jams and preserves, and she knew the instant he inhaled the fragrant aroma of the extensive array of fresh-baked breads and pastry items. Pleased by his reaction, she relaxed a little, but she remained out of sight.

"Your parents would've been so pleased," Rose told him. "It's a shame you sold their house. Where will you live? What about your law practice? What are your plans?" She inspected him from head to foot with critical eyes. "You look too thin to me, Thomas. Are you eating properly? Please tell me you aren't staying in some dreadful motel when I have a perfectly good guest room at my house."

Geneva watched him laugh at the barrage of questions. She wondered if his laughter was low and resonant, then promptly told herself it didn't really matter. She wouldn't ever be able to hear it, anyway.

"You should have been a prosecutor, Aunt Rose."

"I've always made it my policy to leave the lawyering in the family to the men, as out of step as that makes me with what's politically correct these days. Now, tell me exactly what's going on with you."

He shrugged. "It's not complicated. I've cashed out of the partnership."

Rose's smile faded. "You founded that partnership, Thomas, so something serious must have happened."

Under Geneva's watchful eyes, Thomas pondered the observation for several moments before responding. As he stood there, he unzipped his leather jacket to reveal a mauve cableknit sweater that stretched across his broad chest. Shoving his hands into the pockets of black jeans that molded to obviously muscular thighs, he rocked back on the heels of his western boots.

Geneva sucked in a quick breath. She told herself that his physique was no more impressive than any other male in his prime, but she knew she lied. It was easy to see why this ruggedly hewn man had a reputation with women.

"Thomas?"

"A lot of things have happened over the years, Aunt Rose. When they started to add up, I decided it was time for a new beginning. So, here I am."

"You need a life," the older woman said emphatically. "You need to *share* your life. You've been alone too long."

"Maybe."

"There's no maybe about it."

Thomas smiled.

Geneva noticed the tension that invaded his posture, despite his pleasant expression.

"I have plenty of space—" Rose began.

"I'm forty, and I really don't need a keeper."

"You know me too well. I'd fuss you right out of the house, wouldn't I?"

He nodded, his hard-featured face gentled somewhat by his teasing smile. "Probably, but I'm counting on you to feed me once in a while."

"You don't even have to ask." Rose paused for a moment. "I have a wonderful friend in real estate. Shall I call her for you?"

"Let me get my office set up first," he said. "I've got a place to stay for the time being."

"A hotel," Rose said, sniffing her disdain.

"Guilty as charged, ma'am."

He grinned down at her as she shook a finger at him. Geneva liked the affection she saw in his eyes. She'd seen pictures of Rose's extended family. All the men were tall, built with typical western sturdiness, and possessed character-filled faces. Thomas fit the family mold to a T.

"How was Egypt?" he asked.

"Extraordinary, of course!" Rose exclaimed. "It exceeded every expectation I had."

"You always talked about going there."

"And I finally did, thanks to you."

"It was my pleasure, believe me, and a modest thank-you for your support over the years."

"You're family, and I love you," she reminded him as she squeezed his hand. "I'm so glad you're here, but why didn't you tell me about your plans before I left on my trip?"

Geneva took a step back, suddenly feeling very foolish for eavesdropping. Time to stop hiding, she decided.

Geneva stepped into view and immediately felt seared by his gaze. She wore another bodysuit, this one black, and a wraparound fringed leather skirt. As she crossed the room, the leather parted with every step she took to reveal her legs.

Her body responded to the heat that flashed in his eyes. Geneva felt as though she was being caressed by invisible fingertips of flame.

The scorching sensations didn't cease. They kept sizzling through her, making her more aware of herself as a woman than she'd been in several years. She strolled at a relaxed pace, a polite expression on her face as she approached Rose and her nephew. She stepped past Thomas Coltrane to hug her friend. Then she faced them both, although she directed her comments to Rose: "Welcome back. You've been missed."

Rose smiled. She signed, supplementing their introduction by finger-spelling their names. "Geneva Talmadge, this is Thomas Coltrane, my nephew."

Geneva deliberately met his gaze, her chin lifting slightly as she kept her poise in place. "We met yesterday." Her hands wove through the air as she talked. "Unfortunately, I thought he was a masher and treated him accordingly."

Rose darted a what-in-the-world-have-you-done-now glance at Thomas.

He inclined his head. "No harm done. In fact, if I ever need an ally in a tough situation, I know whom to call."

Geneva smiled then, and she gave him points. She loathed being perceived as a helpless deaf woman. "I gather you're moving back to Cedar Grove."

"I already have."

"Welcome home, then."

He extended his hand.

Geneva hesitated briefly. Not to respond, she realized, would be rude. The instant their palms met and mated, Geneva knew she shouldn't have allowed Thomas Coltrane to touch her. His warmth penetrated her skin and she felt as if she'd held her hand too close to a fire.

"I'm glad to meet you under more . . . ideal circumstances," he said.

Although she looked perplexed, Rose signed for him.

"Thank you," Geneva answered, easing free of his grasp. Her eyes remained locked on his face as she searched for motives hidden beneath the surface of polite words and an easy smile. His touch stayed with her, however, unsettling her to such a degree that she frowned—as much at him as at her reaction to him.

"We're neighbors," he remarked.

Geneva glanced at Rose, who continued to sign for her nephew.

"Neighbors?" she clarified, returning her gaze to his face.

Thomas nodded. "I've leased most of the top floor of the building."

She felt her composure slip a notch, but she recovered quickly. "You're an attorney, I believe."

"That's right."

Geneva noticed the uncharacteristic scowl on Rose's face. Her scowl turned into a glare. Even though Thomas seemed indifferent, Geneva couldn't help wondering about the cause of Rose's ire.

"We're a small community and very law-abiding," she remarked.

He smiled easily. "I know. I grew up here."

As she watched his lips, Geneva realized how relaxed and composed he seemed. She envied him his poise. Hers seemed on the verge of deserting her. "Rose speaks of your childhood upon occasion. To hear her tell it, you were quite the hell-raiser."

Rose abruptly excused herself before Thomas could reply. Geneva assumed that the bell above the door had alerted her to the arrival of customers. A glance at the front of the store confirmed her assumption.

She didn't protest when Thomas took her arm and guided her deeper into the store, but she stepped back when he released her. The warmth of his touch lingered. Your reaction to this man is crazy, she told herself, so settle down and deal with him like an adult.

Thomas simultaneously signed and commented, "I didn't mean to frighten you yesterday. I approached you because you looked upset. I thought you might need a friend."

At first surprised by his use of sign language, Geneva remembered what Rose had told her about the loss of hearing Thomas's mother had suffered following a car accident. She gave him a few more points, then told herself that, points or no points, this man was too much of an unknown quantity to let him get too close.

"You didn't frighten me, Mr. Coltrane, but you did startle me," she explained. "I was very preoccupied when you came up behind me, hence my reaction."

His hands, which had signed with some hesitation before, moved with more sureness this time. "Call me Thomas, please. We both know I frightened you, so there's no point in debating the obvious, is there?"

Stiffening, Geneva asked, "How long were you in the hallway?"

"Not long."

She watched his eyes. "Did you overhear the conversation that took place?"

He shrugged. "Not enough to make much sense of it."

She knew instantly that he was lying. She wondered why. His facial expression said he knew that she knew, but he didn't say anything more. She silently applauded him for not compounding one lie with another.

"I trust you'll respect my privacy."

"Of course," he said, looking puzzled that she felt compelled to question his ethics.

Geneva pondered his reaction for a moment. He seemed sincere. "Thank you."

"You're very welcome."

Geneva sensed the predator in Thomas Coltrane, despite his good manners. She knew all about predators, and for Rose's sake, Geneva wanted to assume that he posed no danger. Still, she vowed to be very careful whenever she found herself in his company.

"Rose refers to you in her letters," he remarked.

"You must have been bored."

"Unusual women never bore me. In fact, I'm sorry it's taken me so long to meet you."

Unusual? she thought, wondering exactly what he meant. She didn't inquire, however. Her instincts told her not to bother. "I'm a simple shop owner, Mr. Coltrane."

He chuckled. "Somehow, Ms. Talmadge, I seriously doubt that there's anything even remotely simple about you. Besides, anyone capable of creating a successful business in a tough economic climate has my admiration and respect."

"What kind of law do you plan to practice?" she asked, changing the subject.

He cooperated, but the amusement lighting his eyes assured her that he saw through her ploy. "Any kind that comes my way."

"Cedar Grove already has three attorneys."

"Are you suggesting there isn't room for one more?"

"I'm suggesting that you'll need clients from other communities if you plan to earn a living."

He inclined his head. "Thank you for the warning, but I'm optimistic about my prospects."

"It wasn't a warning, merely a statement of fact." *I sound so prissy*, she thought in frustration.

"You're obviously well versed in the legal needs of the area."

"I'm well versed in the community and its residents. I've lived here for nearly twelve years."

"Perhaps you'd like to act as my unofficial consultant?"

She paused. "I have every confidence that you've already done your homework, so you don't need me."

A sad look appeared on his face.

Geneva wondered why.

"I'm still working on what I need in this life, but that's a conversation best saved for a quiet evening, a good bottle of wine, and a friend."

She stared at him, taken aback by his revealing remark. Most men were reluctant to admit that they didn't have all the answers. Oddly enough, instead of making him seem weak, Thomas Coltrane seemed infinitely stronger and much more human.

He glanced at her left hand. "You aren't married."

"No, I'm not married," she signed, wary once again.

He smiled. "I'm glad, but I'm also surprised."

Geneva cut to the bottom line, as was her habit. "I don't date."

"Why?"

"I just don't."

He studied her for a long moment. "I'm not the enemy, Geneva."

She paled and glanced away when she saw the empathy in his eyes. She didn't like the feeling of vulnerability he summoned from her, so she fought it with every shred of strength she possessed.

He thwarted her. Easily. Effortlessly. He simply reached out, touched her chin with a single fingertip, and gently guided her face so that she could see his mouth and hands.

Unnerved, Geneva took a step backward. "Let me make this easy for you, Mr. Coltrane.

My social life is confined to a small group of established friends. I'm the co-owner of Talmadge, Inc., and I live a simple life. I intend to keep it that way. End of story."

"Simple. There's that word again."

"Simple," she confirmed.

"I don't think so."

"Mr. Coltrane—"

"Thomas," he reminded her yet again as his gaze traveled over her face. "Please."

She sucked in a quick breath, then told herself to relax. She studied his rugged face with equal thoroughness, though, searching for what, she didn't know.

And as she stood there, she suddenly imagined what it might be like to spend quiet winter evenings in front of a roaring fire with this man. She imagined sharing confidences, laughter, even a snifter of brandy after a leisurely meal. She imagined what she always imagined, although she usually did it when she was alone. She imagined the luxury of sharing her life with a man who valued her above all things.

Geneva belatedly noticed the slow darkening of his thickly lashed, hazel eyes. She noticed, too, the muscle that throbbed in his cheek. Her gaze shifted briefly to his long-fingered hands before returning to his face. She let herself fantasize for the briefest of moments about what it would feel like to have his hands skimming over her body. She felt her insides quiver with a sensation akin to anticipation that shook her to her soul. The woman concealed behind the polite manner of a shopkeeper seemed determined to emerge. With Jamal dead and buried, her prison term had ended.

Her father had once warned her about passion, saying that the right man would come along someday and she wouldn't know what hit her. She was, he'd insisted, like her mother, but Geneva only vaguely remembered Erin Talmadge, while Patrick had often waxed poetic about the remarkable woman he'd loved and then lost to wanderlust and neglect. She hadn't understood his comments at sixteen. She did now.

Geneva wondered if Thomas was tender or aggressive in his passion with a woman, or some combination of the two. Would his heart race or would he always remain in control, as he was now? Was he all skill and finesse, or did his emotions overwhelm him and his heartbeat throb in his fingertips when he made love?

"You have remarkably expressive eyes," he signed.

She blinked in surprise, then chastised herself for letting her thoughts go off on such an erotic tangent.

A sigh escaped Geneva, a shattered sound

that spoke of loneliness too long endured, of fantasies never fulfilled, and of the longing to be desired and loved.

Thomas studied her for a moment, then said, "You arouse my curiosity, Geneva Talmadge."

She moistened her lower lip with the tip of her tongue. "Curiosity?"

"It's hard to explain." His gaze snagged on her lips. "I have the feeling that you're as lonely and isolated as I've been in recent years."

"You're assuming a great deal, aren't you?"

"I don't think so, but you tell me. Am I wrong?"

Honesty and self-defense warred within her. Honesty won. "I'm committed to my work."

He nodded, his expression becoming bleak. "Ditto. It's not enough, is it?"

She trembled, fighting the pull of his presence and his unexpected candor, fighting the desire stirring in her heart and body, fighting him, although he really didn't seem to realize the tumultuous state of her emotional response to him. For that small favor, she said a silent prayer of thanks.

"I—" she began.

"You don't have to say anything," he signed without speaking. "And I apologize if

I've made you uncomfortable. That wasn't my intention."

She stared at him, drawn to him despite her uncertainty and confusion.

"I'd like to get to know you."

"We're working in the same building," she pointed out.

"I was thinking more along the lines of friendship."

"Why?"

"You're an unusual woman."

Geneva stiffened, old reflexes that were impossible to fight at that moment shooting to the surface. "I'm hearing impaired, and I own a business. There's nothing unusual about that."

Thomas shook his head, clearly dismayed. "That isn't what I meant, and you know it."

Geneva suddenly craved space and privacy. "Enjoy your new life, Thomas Coltrane."

"Don't run from me. There's no need."

"I'm not running," Geneva insisted, then felt stupid for lying.

He exhaled.

She watched the rise and fall of his broad shoulders before refocusing on his face. She caught a glimpse of the compassion she'd seen earlier, and it softened her resistance.

Before she could speak, he glanced past her. The transformation of his features, from compassionate stranger to steely eyed observer, gave her pause.

Geneva jerked with shock when a hand settled on her shoulder a second later. Her discomfort turned to relief, though, when she turned to the person who'd touched her, recognized him, and stepped forward into his arms without hesitation. She held fast to him, as though he represented a lifeline.

Thomas recognized the man, too. He knew better than to overreact. He reminded himself that he had no rights where Geneva Talmadge was concerned, especially not the right to be jealous. But he was, and the emotion stunned him.

"Nicholas," she whispered.

Thomas heard the relief in Geneva's low voice. The resentment he felt stabbed at him like a sharp blade as he met and held the gaze of the newcomer.

"How are you, little one?" Nicholas asked once she stepped back from him. He assessed Thomas, his expression enigmatic.

"Adjusting," she quipped, but her attempt at lightheartedness sounded strained and drew a frown from both men.

Thomas watched her struggle for composure. He understood how she felt, although for very different reasons.

"You'll be fine," Nicholas assured her. "You've always been tougher than you look."

Unwilling to back away, Thomas stepped forward and extended his hand. "Thomas Coltrane."

"Rose's nephew," Nicholas confirmed as they shook hands.

"That's right."

"San Diego attorney-at-law, if I'm not mistaken."

"*Former* San Diego attorney."

"Nick Benteen, longtime resident of Cedar Grove and sometime author," he offered.

You're a hell of a lot more than that, Thomas thought, his gaze direct and unflinching.

THREE

Geneva watched the two strong-willed, single-minded men silently assess each other. She'd learned long ago about the territorial nature of males, and nothing they did surprised her any longer.

While Geneva felt strengthened by Nicholas's presence, she experienced a moment of compassion for Thomas, then a surge of satisfaction when he seemed unintimidated by her self-appointed guardian. Most people felt compelled to turn tail and run if Nicholas paused to scrutinize them, but not Thomas Coltrane.

"Welcome back to Cedar Grove." Nicholas automatically signed in order to include Geneva in the conversation. "I understand you're one of my new tenants."

Thomas signed as well, despite his visible

surprise at the news that the building they stood in was owned by Nicholas Benteen. "That's right. I signed the lease yesterday."

Geneva decided it was time to step in. She didn't even question the impulse; she simply acted on it. "Where are Hannah and the baby today?"

Nicholas smiled at the mention of his wife and infant daughter. "They're still with the pediatrician." He glanced at his watch. "Time for me to head in that direction. I had a couple of minutes, though, and I wanted to check on you." His gaze swept over her with characteristic thoroughness.

Geneva knew the drill, so she humored him. "One day at a time . . ." she began, recalling the motto Nicholas had urged her to adopt shortly after losing her hearing.

". . . and life works," he finished for her.

Geneva found comfort in the familiar patter. The words they spoke might have seemed clichéd to most people, she realized, but they symbolized the philosophy that guided her life.

Nicholas extended his hand to Thomas for a parting handshake. "Good to meet you. If you have any problems with the office space, let the property manager handle them for you. Geneva's a great resource when it comes to the local business community. She was the president of the Business League last year."

Geneva's smile slipped. Nicholas normally didn't encourage anyone to seek her out, and she wondered why he'd made an exception with Thomas Coltrane. Her smile reappeared when he tapped the end of her nose with his fingertip. She felt his affection, the depth of his friendship, and the courage he so willingly shared in the playful gesture.

Returning her attention to Thomas once Nicholas departed, she signed, "I need to get back to work. I'm up to my eyeballs in paperwork."

"I understand."

She paused, then expressed a sincere thought. "I hope you'll be happy with your new life."

"I'm counting on it."

His serious expression prompted her to remark, "You are, aren't you?"

"Very much."

As she looked at him, her instinctive resistance to Thomas Coltrane lessened even more. She grasped the challenges inherent in making major life changes. Grasped them far more than she wanted to admit to anyone, including herself.

"You'll make it happen," she encouraged.

"Wish me luck?"

She smiled, then nodded. As she met his gaze, she realized that Thomas, by simply walking into her store that morning, had reinforced her awareness that she needed more than a small circle of friends and a successful business to be happy. She needed what she'd dreamed of so often, what her father had called a partner of the soul—a man capable of being a lover, friend, ally, and confidant.

Geneva knew she had to find a way to release herself from the bondage of restraint and reserve that had ruled her existence for so many years, but she still wondered if she would ever achieve the acceptance and mutual trust she sought in a loving relationship. The possibility of rejection existed, and Thomas Coltrane made her very aware of the enormous risk inherent in revealing the truth of her past.

"What's wrong, Geneva?" he signed.

She flushed. "Nothing, really. Help yourself to preserves if you'd like to sample our wares," she invited, producing her best shopkeeper-dealing-with-a-customer smile. "We're known for our natural ingredients."

"I'm a good listener, if you'd like to talk."

"Thank you, but—"

"I know how tough it can be to confide in anyone, let alone a stranger, but I'm available if you change your mind."

"I'm sure you mean well, Thomas."

"I do, but I also have a motive," he admitted.

"Which is?" she asked guardedly.

"I meant it when I said I'd like to get to know you."

Be honest, she told herself. You're curious about him, too. "I'd like to get to know you, but not all at once. I can't move that fast with anyone."

He smiled. "Your pace, and your rules. Scout's honor."

He means it, she realized. "I'm like a snail," she cautioned.

His smile turned to laughter.

Once again, she wished she could have heard the sound, if only for a moment.

"I'm not, but I'll adjust."

"Take care of yourself."

"You, too."

Geneva started to turn away, but she paused when she felt his fingers close around her wrist. She darted a glance in his direction, then drew in a steadying breath to counteract the impact of his touch. But like before, the warmth of his fingertips stayed with her long after he released her.

"Are you really all right?"

"Of course."

Something in his expression told her that he didn't completely believe her.

"You're a beautiful woman."

Startled, she said, "Thank you."

Other men had made the same observation, but she'd always dismissed their remarks.

Geneva realized she didn't want to dismiss anything associated with this particular man.

"You've known Benteen for some time, haven't you?"

She nodded, wariness filtering into her.

"He's very protective of you."

"He's my friend."

"I'm glad. Real friends are few and far between."

That surprised her. "So is his wife," she said, willing to clarify a situation that puzzled many of the local townspeople. "Nicholas is the big brother I never had. I . . . I trust him."

"Trust is very important."

Geneva nodded. "It's everything."

"It's an integral element of any successful relationship."

"I agree," she said.

"I want your trust."

She felt her heart trip to a momentary stop. "Why?"

"Friendship isn't possible without it."

"Trust takes time, especially between men and women."

"Will you give me the time, or were you just being polite before?"

He's asking for more than time, she realized. She wanted time, too. Time to get to know him. Time to figure out if she was reacting to him out of pure loneliness. "You're asking for more than you know, but I'm willing to try."

"I'm asking for an opportunity, that's all."

An opportunity to do what? she wondered. *Seduce me? Stop being so cynical*, a voice in her head scolded. *You like him, even though he unnerves the hell out of you.*

She thought then about some of the things she already knew about him. "You have a reputation, you know."

He grinned, the boyishness of his expression reaching into his hazel eyes so that they almost sparkled with mischief. She very nearly grinned back at him, but she managed not to.

"You shouldn't believe everything you read in the tabloids."

Her eyes widened. "I was referring to things Rose has told me about you."

"Damn. I spoke too soon."

"Tabloids?" she finger-spelled as she said the word.

"I'm afraid so."

Geneva sobered. "I've been alone for several years."

"Me, too," he said, his humor fading.

"I don't want to . . ." Make a mistake in judgment, she almost said, but she managed to still her tongue before she sounded like a preadolescent trying to protect her diginity.

Thomas read her thoughts. "I don't want to make a mistake, either. It's why I haven't gotten emotionally entangled with anyone since my divorce."

He doesn't want to be hurt, she realized, surprised anew by his candor.

"Think about it," he encouraged, clasping her slender hand between both of his.

His warmth seeped into her skin. Again.

Her pulse raced. Again.

He trailed his fingertips over the inside of her wrist.

She knew by the slight flaring of his nostrils that he felt her response to him. She exhaled, hoping her shakiness wasn't too evident.

Geneva withdrew her hand, grateful that he was gentleman enough not to push. She followed his gaze as it traveled over the store. Additional customers had arrived, but Rose didn't seem overwhelmed.

"This place reminds me of my mother's pantry. Only much larger, of course."

Geneva asked, "You have good memories of your childhood, don't you?"

He smiled. "The best."

"You're very fortunate."

His smile evaporated. "I know."

Geneva looked away, feeling awkward because she knew she'd just revealed a fact about her life that she usually kept concealed.

"What do you recommend?" he asked when she looked at him again.

Geneva didn't respond. She wasn't certain about his meaning.

Thomas gestured at the jars of preserves and woven baskets filled with baked breads and pastries.

She resurrected her poise. "Everything, but if you happen to be partial to preserves, I recommend the strawberry and raspberry."

"Are they your personal favorites?" Thomas asked.

"Yes. They were my first two creations, and they took forever to perfect."

Geneva felt tremendous pride as she glanced around. The business that had begun as a form of self-therapy several years earlier had evolved into such a success, a conglomerate had approached her with a lucrative deal. They wanted to create a nationwide chain of retail outlets patterned after her shop and introduce her products to the international market. The transition from building explosive devices to creating recipes for jams and preserves still amazed her.

"I have a definite weakness for raspberry," Thomas confessed.

She laughed, feeling like a coconspirator. "Me, too. Whatever you choose, though, I promise you won't be disappointed."

Thomas fell silent for a lengthy moment. "I don't think you could disappoint me, Geneva. Not ever."

She stared at him, struck by the intimate connotation of his comment. It reached into her heart to tempt and tantalize.

Thomas answered Rose's front door early the next evening.

Nonplussed for a moment, Geneva scrambled to gather her wits. "Rose invited me to supper."

"I know. I wangled an invitation, too."

"I don't imagine you had to twist her arm. She has a low opinion of hotel food."

He stepped aside. "Come on in. You look chilled."

She wiped her feet on the mat before stepping inside, then placed her shoulder bag on a nearby bench. "I think we're supposed to get more snow tonight."

"The ski crowd will be delighted."

"The local merchants, as well. Since the army closed the base eight years ago, Cedar Grove has come to depend on the revenue brought in by winter sports."

Thomas took her jacket after she shrugged free of it. He placed it on the bench next to her purse. "How about a glass of wine? I've just uncorked a bottle of Chenin Blanc that I've been saving for a special occasion."

"Please. Homecomings should always be celebrated." Geneva preceded Thomas into the spacious country-style kitchen she'd visited many times before.

"You're just in time," Rose said and signed after she deposited a platter on the table already set for three.

Geneva smiled, although still a bit unsettled that Rose hadn't bothered to mention that she'd invited Thomas to join them for dinner. "I've brought an appetite."

"Excellent, especially since Thomas badgered me into fixing his favorite meal, and I always double the quantity when I prepare it for him."

"Veal piccata." His delight obvious, he handed Geneva a half-filled wineglass. "The woman is a genius with veal."

Geneva took a sip of the Chenin Blanc. "Do you need any help, Rose?"

"Absolutely not. If I know you, you've been on your feet since before dawn. You two sit yourselves down and start on your salads. I'll be right with you. I just have to get the rolls out of the oven."

Geneva did as instructed. "You worked today, too," she reminded her.

"For seven whole hours." The older woman smiled. "Which is nothing compared to your sixteen-hour days, young lady."

Thomas remained standing. "Every day?" he asked.

"Yes," Rose supplied when Geneva hesitated. "Every single day. She's just like you. A total workaholic."

Geneva laughed. She couldn't help herself. Rose mothered everyone. Being her employer didn't exempt her from maternal concern or periodic chastisements, but she didn't mind. The concern warmed her. "I'm not quite that compulsive."

Thomas drew out Rose's chair for her when she joined them at the table a few moments later.

Rose patted his arm. "You're still a lady killer with good manners, I see." Glancing at Geneva, she said, "His mother and I used to despair about the young women who threw themselves at him. His ego had already gone through the roof by the time he was sixteen."

Thomas chuckled. "Rose is overstating her case. I was a pretty shy kid."

"That didn't stop the girls," Rose countered.

Geneva's smile faded. Guarding her heart was an old habit, one she obviously shouldn't abandon in the near future, she decided. Some men were into trophies, and she certainly didn't plan to be an addition to the Thomas Coltrane collection.

"Don't believe everything she tells you," he advised. "I'm a firm believer in quality, not quantity."

Geneva almost dropped the serving dish of veal she'd just picked up.

Thomas gave her an amused look. "Let me hold that for you while you serve yourself." He relieved her of the heavy platter, still smiling at her.

Geneva concentrated on her food, allowing Rose and Thomas the luxury of reminiscing about past times. They included her in their conversation by signing at all times. She asked several questions, but she was halfway through her meal before she loosened up enough to start tasting the food she was putting into her mouth.

They lingered over dessert and coffee, but the lateness of the hour finally prompted Geneva and Rose to clear the table. Over Thomas's protests, the women banished him from the kitchen so that they could do the dishes. He didn't reappear until it was time to walk out to their individual vehicles.

"You seem more relaxed," he observed.

Seated in her car, Geneva finished securing her seat belt before she answered him. "I am now, but Rose didn't mention you were joining us for dinner when she invited me."

"I asked her not to."

"Why?" she signed.

He leaned down, studying her through the open window. "I didn't think you'd join us if you knew I'd be here. I was right, wasn't I?"

She shrugged. "Maybe."

"Is this just a simple case of shyness? Or is something else going on with you that I should know about?"

"I don't like surprises, Thomas. I've always had an aversion to being manipulated, even for the best of reasons."

Geneva spoke in that breathlessly low voice that Thomas knew he would hear for the rest of his life. "I won't forget that," he promised.

"Please don't."

"How about lunch tomorrow?"

"I'll have to check my calendar," she said. Was he asking her for a date? She hadn't had a real date since her early twenties.

"Let me know."

She nodded. "I will."

"Drive safely." He straightened and stepped back.

Geneva rolled up the car window and turned the key in the ignition. Nothing happened. She tried again. Dead silence. Not tonight, she thought in frustration.

Thomas opened the door. "Problem?"

"Unfortunately." She released her seat belt and got out of the Jeep. "I need to check under the hood."

"You create designer preserves *and* you repair car engines?"

If you only knew, she thought as she nodded. Her mechanical skills and proficiency with technical details had been apparent since childhood. She'd constructed entire towns with multiple Erector sets, solved every electrical problem that came up when she combined several train kits, and excelled at math.

Thomas stopped her before she took a single step. "It's dark out, and it's snowing again. Let's deal with this in the morning. I'll drive you home tonight."

Geneva hesitated, then noticed Rose, who stood under the front porch light. The older woman lifted her hands and signed, "Car trouble again?"

Geneva confirmed Rose's query with a thumbs-up gesture.

"What does she mean, 'again'?" Thomas asked.

"The starter's been giving me fits this winter."

"Thomas, tell Geneva that I'll notify the garage. They can come out first thing in the morning," Rose called out before disappearing inside her house and turning off the front porch light.

"I guess that's settled," he remarked. "Come on, let's get you home. With the hours you apparently keep, you need your rest."

He hustled her into the front seat of his car before she could voice a protest. Feeling uneasy at the prospect of being alone with Thomas, Geneva fastened her seat belt and gripped the leather shoulder bag in her lap.

He reached out to touch her hand. "I don't bite."

She met his gaze and saw only concern, but she stubbornly refused to acknowledge it. "It's late."

Nodding, he started the car.

Other than to direct Thomas down a series of country roads cast in total darkness, Geneva said little during the twenty-minute drive. She felt a little foolish for being so terse with him, but her nerves had gotten the best of her. She couldn't remember the last time she'd been in a car with a man who wasn't a part of her close-knit family of friends. Relieved that Thomas had to keep his hands on the steering wheel—it eliminated his ability to sign and therefore talk to her—Geneva finally did relax.

They traveled deeper and deeper into the dense forest that edged the town of Cedar Grove. She didn't bother to explain that Nicholas Benteen owned virtually every acre they traversed.

Thomas pulled into the newly plowed circular drive in front of the three-story cedar chalet Geneva called home. She'd designed it herself, her need to have a permanent home the result of years of gypsy-like wandering with her late father.

Once he turned off the car engine, Thomas asked, "The evening wasn't so bad, was it?"

She shook her head. "My social skills are a tad rusty, I'm afraid."

"We can change that, Geneva."

She expressed the doubt she felt. "I'm not sure change, real change, is always possible, even when it's wanted."

"Why don't we test the possibility? I've already promised to honor any rules you want to establish."

"That's not your style."

He smiled. "True, but you're worth the effort."

"How can you know that?"

"Instinct, pure and simple."

"You can be very charming and persuasive when you put your mind to it."

"My secret's out, I see."

Geneva signed, "Thank you for driving me home."

Before he could stop her, she slipped out of the car and started up the shoveled path that led to the deck encircling her house like an apron. A gust of cold air buffeted her body and tugged at her hair as she walked, but she hardly felt the subzero temperature.

Geneva's footsteps triggered motion sensors that illuminated her property. Stately centuries-old pine trees, the branches frosted with fresh snow, swayed in the moonlight on either side of the chalet and gave the area an ethereal appearance.

Although she didn't hear the crunch of snow beneath his booted feet, she sensed that Thomas was only a few yards behind her as she climbed the wide cedar staircase and crossed the deck to the front door. With every step she took she felt an almost palpable need to reach out to him, to take the first step toward some semblance of a normal life.

She paused a few feet from the door, drew in a steadying breath, and turned to look at him.

"You're afraid of me."

She knew he wasn't asking. He was telling.

She felt foolish. She also felt a little defensive. "Your imagination is getting the best of you."

"I don't think so."

"Thomas . . ."

He reached out, his fingertips gentle as he stroked the side of her face for a brief moment. "You don't have anything to fear from me."

But she was afraid. Afraid to let herself want too much. Afraid to dream. Afraid of the confusing feelings and fragile emotions he roused in her. Geneva edged backward. The front door stopped her, though. Squaring her shoulders, she lifted her hands. "I'm very tired."

"Please don't shut me out," he signed.

"I need to think."

"Why don't you just let yourself feel, instead?"

"You make it sound so simple."

"Nothing important is simple. We're both old enough to know that, but we're also both old enough to realize that there's something happening between us. Something I don't quite understand, either, but something worth exploring."

Geneva briefly pressed the fingertips of both hands to her suddenly throbbing temples. "I'm not afraid."

"Then what are you?" he asked.

"Nervous," she blurted out.

He smiled, looking relieved. "Me, too."

"And very inexperienced."

"I probably have enough experience for both of us."

She laughed at his rueful expression. She couldn't help herself. "That's one of the reasons I'm so tense around you."

Thomas took one of her hands and brought it to his lips. He pressed a kiss into the center of her palm, the tip of his tongue painting a swath of moist flame over her skin.

She felt her heart stutter, then slam against

her ribs at a hard gallop. Eyes wide, she met his gaze.

Reaching up, she stroked his hard cheek with shaking fingertips, unable to stop herself from seeking the warmth of his skin. The feel of the stubble that covered the lower half of his face tantalized her.

Thomas exhaled raggedly, his eyes so dark they appeared black as Geneva stared up at him. "How long has it been since you've been with a man?"

She blinked, startled by his bluntness. She decided that she must have misunderstood his question.

Thomas persisted. "How long has it been since you've trusted anyone other than that small circle of friends you mentioned when we were talking yesterday?"

"Forever," she admitted after several moments of silence.

"Have you taken a lover in all that time?"

Geneva balked. "That's none of your business."

"You've just answered my question."

"Good night, Thomas. I'll get a ride into town in the morning with a *friend*." She started to turn away from him.

He settled his large hands on her shoulders to stop her. "Don't be embarrassed."

"I'm not."

"Then what are you feeling right now?"

"Annoyance!" Geneva gave him a belligerent look, then tried to jerk free.

He held her still. "You're special, and you don't even realize it, do you?"

Special? Perplexed, she asked the obvious. "Why?"

"For so many reasons, I don't even know where to begin." A heartbeat later, he lowered his head and took her lips.

Geneva went absolutely still with shock.

Thomas tenderly kissed her, nibbling at her lips, then laving the width of them with the tip of his tongue. He didn't try to seduce her in the moments that followed. He tried, instead, to express his sincerity, his commitment not to rush or use her.

He felt the tremors that moved through her, felt the strength in her slender fingers a moment later when she gripped his forearms, and then he inhaled the shaken breath that flowed past her lips. He exercised every shred of control he'd ever acquired as he gently explored her.

He tasted heat and inexperience. He tasted hunger and hesitation. And he tasted sensuality tempered by anxiety, the latter emotion sending a surge of compassion through him.

He wanted more from her than a simple kiss. He craved much more, but even though his body clamored for the ultimate possession, he knew better than to rush Geneva. He would only end up regretting such behavior. So instead he gathered her into a loose embrace and plied her lips with the gentlest, most reverent of kisses.

Geneva responded. Cautiously at first, then with curiosity.

He knew the instant the barriers started to shatter, not just the barrier that had cordoned off her emotions, but also the one that had shielded his own heart for a very long time. Emotions he hadn't felt in years mingled with his desire for her, emotions that made him want to cherish this woman.

Geneva parted her lips, welcoming the teasing forays of his tongue. Angling her head, she allowed him to deepen their kiss, then gasped when Thomas invaded the heated recesses of her mouth.

She moaned.

Thomas drank in the erotic sound. His pulse kicked into high gear. Framing her face with his hands, he explored every curve and ridge beyond the boundary of her lips.

The soft sounds she made seduced him. He lingered over her, sipping at times, penetrating deeply when his restraint unraveled, slowing himself down when it became necessary, all the while savoring the taste of her. Too soon, his body began clamoring for more than he knew she could offer.

He couldn't violate her trust. She would hate him if he did. And he would hate himself.

Trailing his lips across her cheek, Thomas nuzzled her neck, then nipped at the delicate, fragrant skin there as he tried to cool down. After a while he lifted his head and peered at her, the burning in his bloodstream still painful, but very much under control.

The disbelief and desire he glimpsed in her huge blue eyes made him want to carry her off to the nearest bed. Instead, he released her and said, "You'd better get inside. I'll see you tomorrow."

Looking dazed, Geneva nodded.

He watched her let herself into the chalet before he made his way back to his car and drove to his hotel.

By dawn the next morning, Thomas Coltrane knew exactly what his next move would be.

FOUR

Early one morning the following week, a helicopter touched down on the snow-covered landing area adjacent to Geneva's property.

She didn't feel alarmed. She recognized the distinctive blue-and-gray chopper, but she lingered at the window, anyway. Once she confirmed the identity of the pilot, she made her way to the kitchen, turned on the coffeemaker, and then walked to the front door.

She greeted Nicholas with a smile. "You're up early."

He grinned as he pulled off gloves and a knit cap and shoved them into his jacket pocket. "Haven't you ever heard the old cliché 'there's no rest for the wicked'?"

She gave him an amused look. "I thought that was 'for the weary,'" she signed, then glanced at the snow melting at his feet.

"Don't forget to take off your boots. I'm not inclined to mop up your snow puddles."

He removed both his jacket and heavy boots. "You sound just like Hannah."

"Great minds think alike," she said with a laugh. "Coffee's on. Come into the kitchen."

Nicholas followed her down the wide hallway and into the glass-walled kitchen. A huge room, it had been the original site of her preserve-making endeavors. The fragrance of fresh herbs and spices scented the air, blending with the smell of roasted coffee beans.

Nicholas filled a mug, then downed almost half the contents before speaking again. "It's cold out this morning."

"It's cold *and* early," Geneva responded. "To what do I owe the honor?"

"I need a favor."

"Name it, but why didn't you just use the computer or the fax machine?" she asked. "You could have saved yourself the trip."

He hesitated, then confessed. "This is above and beyond the call of duty."

"Do tell." Geneva filled a mug for herself and sipped the steaming brew.

"I'm taking Hannah and the baby to Saint Louis. Her parents are celebrating their fiftieth wedding anniversary this coming weekend."

"Is Sean going with you?" she asked, referring to her partner and his brother-in-law.

Nicholas shook his head. "He's not into crowds yet. We'll be bringing the folks back with us, so he'll see them when they're here."

Despite the easy flow of conversation, Geneva sensed his discomfort. And it had nothing whatsoever to do with Sean.

Geneva set down her mug. "You visit Saint Louis quite regularly, so what's different about this trip? And why is the favor you need above and beyond the call of duty?"

"I have a potential buyer for the lodge, and I'd like you to represent my interests while I'm gone. Whoever purchases the lodge and the land surrounding it will be your neighbor, so you have a personal stake in the transaction."

Geneva signed, "Acting as your representative won't be a problem, Nicholas, but you must realize that I trust your judgment. I know you won't sell to just anyone."

"I think it might be a problem for you, but I want you to do this for me, anyway."

Her smile faded. "Why will it be a problem?"

"Tom Coltrane's the prospective buyer."

Tom? "When did you two become so chummy?"

"We've been talking for the last few days. And we aren't exactly chummy, although we do understand each other."

"Ah, male bonding."

He chuckled. "Not quite."

"Why don't you have Sam handle it for you? He is, after all, a real estate attorney."

"I would, but he's in Reno on a case, and he'll be tied up for several weeks."

"Nicholas, don't scheme," she cautioned.

He looked mildly chagrined by her remark. "Hannah said the same thing."

"Smart woman."

"Look, you already know that I think you need to open yourself up to life."

"Playing Cupid won't work, no matter how well intentioned the effort."

"You like him."

She frowned. "Yes, I like him, now that we've begun to get acquainted, but there are boundary lines that I have to enforce for reasons you and I both understand."

"I'm not trying to set you up. I promise."

"Not everyone finds what you've found with Hannah," she reminded him.

Nicholas shrugged. "Maybe, maybe not."

Geneva knew there was nothing casual about this man, so his pretense of innocence didn't ring true.

"If it'll set your mind to rest, I've done an extensive background check on Coltrane."

Startled, she asked, "When? And why, for heaven's sake?"

"He's a tenant in one of my properties."

She nodded. Of course he'd done a background check. Nicholas was as thorough as the day was long, especially when it concerned the safety of his friends and the security of his property.

"I'd forgotten about that."

"He's as clean as a whistle, Geneva. Impeccable reputation, respected in the legal profession, known to be ruthless in court, well liked by his friends and former law partners, divorced for nearly seven years now, excellent credit rating, an investment portfolio that rivals mine. And he keeps himself in great shape, which gives him an added edge."

"An edge?" She exhaled in frustration. "You mean in the unlikely event that he has to defend me?"

"The thought occurred to me. I don't want you vulnerable, not ever."

Nicholas might not want her to be vulnerable, but she was and in ways that would probably surprise him. She suddenly craved an end to this conversation. "If you promise to keep your hands off my personal life, I'll represent your interests."

"Thanks," he said, his relief apparent. "Tom will be here in an hour or so. I checked the road to the lodge during my descent. It's clear, so you won't have any problems getting over there, and you already have a set of keys for the place."

Geneva nodded, feeling uneasy and excited

at the prospect of seeing Thomas again. She always felt that combination of delight and anxiety when they were together, whether in her office sharing a midmorning cup of coffee or across the table from each other at a local lunch spot. He intrigued, he charmed, and he aroused, and he did all those things while also acting like a perfect gentleman.

"Promise me, Nicholas. Please."

Rather than respond, he drained the last of his coffee, then preceded her out of the kitchen and down the hallway to the front door. After stepping into his boots and donning his outerwear, he continued to sidestep the promise she sought and advised, "Don't be afraid to live, little one."

"Nicholas . . ."

He left her standing in the open doorway. Exasperated, she watched him jog the short distance to his helicopter. He lifted off within minutes. She muttered a word she never used unless she was alone, then slammed the front door.

Geneva couldn't recall ever feeling so transparent emotionally. She didn't know whether to laugh or cry.

In the end, she did neither. She simply accepted the fact that her friend and protector had drawn certain conclusions after seeing her with Thomas. Accurate conclusions, she admitted to herself. Conclusions that shouldn't have surprised her at all, because Nicholas also understood from recent personal experience the volatile chemistry and emotional hunger that can rise up between a man and a woman and engulf them when they least expect it.

Geneva recalled with a smile the way in which Hannah had unwittingly stormed the fortress that surrounded Nicholas's heart while on a mission to find her missing brother a few years earlier. Nicholas had fought a valiant battle, but he'd lost. He'd won in the end, though, because in Hannah he'd gained a soul mate.

She envied Nicholas and Hannah. They symbolized the ultimate in a passionate, loving partnership, but Geneva knew in her heart that their relationship was unique. Sighing, she told herself that she couldn't afford to be unrealistic about her own expectations or prospects. Soul mates were a rare commodity.

She bathed and dressed, but her thoughts, the same thoughts that had kept her awake most every night, remained centered on Thomas Coltrane. Whenever they were together, she couldn't stop herself from reliving the kiss they'd shared at her front door.

He'd shocked her, and then he'd aroused her as he lingered at her lips. She'd responded, against her will at first and then with a total absence of restraint. How could she not have responded given the depth of her desire for this man?

She'd felt more than desire, though. She'd experienced a sense of rightness in his embrace that she'd never known with a man before. And profound relief that she was capable of expressing her passion.

Years lived alone had made her anxious about her ability ever to really feel again. She now felt a great deal of thanks to Thomas Coltrane, but she longed for far more than just the physical act of possession. She wanted the fantasy: to be loved and accepted, unconditionally.

A part of Geneva welcomed the possibility of change in her well-guarded life, but another part, the one that feared rejection, urged her to refrain from acting impulsively. Still, she doubted that her heart would be inclined to listen to common sense. She'd been alone too long.

When she returned to the first floor she noticed the blinking light on the sensor panel by the front door. Peering out the living room window, she spotted Thomas Coltrane standing at the railing of the front deck. His attention had been captured by the panoramic view of jagged mountain peaks in the distance and the snow-laden valley at the bottom of the steep incline that fronted her property.

Geneva put on her heavy parka and leather

gloves, tucked the lodge key ring into her pocket, then made her way outside to join him. She promised herself that their conversation would be about real estate. Nothing else.

He turned at the sound of her footsteps.

Her promise to herself faded when she saw the warmth in his gaze. She wanted him so much that she struggled not to walk straight into his arms. She glimpsed his desire for her, but she saw other emotions in his gaze, as well. Restraint. Uncertainty. A hint of vulnerability. Hope. All the things she'd been feeling during the last several days. She silently prayed that her own emotions weren't as apparent.

She slowed to a stop, almost like a doe who scented the potential for jeopardy if she misstepped. Raising a shaking hand, Geneva smoothed back tendrils of hair trying to escape her French braid.

He spoke first. "Good morning."

"I understand you'd like a tour of the lodge."

He nodded.

She felt his gaze quickly skim over her, but her body reacted to the visual caress nonetheless. Despite the control she attempted to exert over herself, Geneva trembled.

"You look rested," he said.

Geneva refused to admit that thoughts of

him had kept her awake yet again. "I slept like a rock."

"I didn't."

She watched him closely, and waited for him to finish.

"I can't seem to get you out of my head," Thomas said. "I haven't been able to since the first time I saw you."

"No one's ever said anything like that to me before, and I don't know how to respond," she answered truthfully.

"Then the men you've known must have been blind."

"I haven't known that many men," she reminded him.

"Then I guess some comments don't require a response," Thomas conceded.

"But you want one, don't you?"

He smiled. "Eventually, but not yet. I don't want to rush you."

Careful, she counseled herself. Repartee with a man who tantalized her wasn't her strong suit, so she settled for honesty. "I've never allowed anyone to rush me, Thomas. Not ever."

"You're obviously a woman who knows her own mind."

"What I am is a woman who trusts her instincts."

Thomas nodded, but he didn't speak right away.

Geneva searched his face in the silent moments that followed, and she realized then that she needed him to be the man she now believed him to be—a man of honor and integrity. Nicholas had implied that Thomas Coltrane was those things and more. So had Rose, but Geneva still hesitated.

She lacked the experience of her peers, women in their mid-thirties who'd had a few relationships, and she felt at a disadvantage. So she felt compelled to proceed with caution, in spite of her clamoring senses.

Thomas finally observed, "Instincts are powerful resources, but only when they aren't used destructively."

"That's been my experience," Geneva answered, then shifted to the purpose of his visit. "Shall we head over to the lodge now? I'm sure you're eager to see it."

"Sounds like a plan."

As Thomas drove, Geneva's gaze lingered on his hands, her imagination producing a seductive image that sent heat rushing into her bloodstream. She saw his palms and long fingers gliding over her skin, molding and shaping her body as he explored it at his leisure, then his fingertips skimming over the curving fullness of her breasts before plucking gently at her nipples.

Lost in the eroticism of her thoughts, she

jumped when Thomas placed his hand on her knee to regain her attention.

"Easy. You're wound awfully tight all of a sudden."

She flushed, then felt like a fool. Looking out the window, she realized why he'd stopped his car. "Take the left fork."

He did as she directed, although she noticed that he darted several glances her way as he slowly navigated the narrow lane. "The lodge is around the next bend in the road," she signed, forcing herself to move beyond the fantasies her mind insisted on producing.

Thomas parked in front of the rustic-looking lodge. A large two-story cedar dwelling with a sloping roof, which was dusted white from the previous night's snowfall, the lodge and spacious pine-tree-studded lot on which it sat reminded him of a Currier and Ives greeting card.

"The photo Nick faxed to me didn't do this place justice." Thomas pushed open his car door and got out.

Nick? Geneva shook her head in disbelief. She accepted his hand when he came around to her side and opened her door. "It's one of the most beautiful homes in the area," she signed as they stood side by side. "Nicholas gave the architect who designed it carte blanche."

"How long has it been empty?" Thomas asked as they climbed the steps to the veranda.

"About a year. The former tenants prefer the tropics, and they live in the Caribbean now."

"Nick didn't mention he'd used the lodge as a rental."

"He didn't. Jean and Mark had a ninety-nine-year lease on the property, but they relinquished it when they left the area."

"What about your place?"

She hesitated, then thought, *In for a penny, in for a pound.* "I have the same arrangement with Nicholas, but I have the option of purchasing the chalet and the land around it at any time. I'm not in a hurry, though. The current arrangement is fine with me."

"Interesting."

"Practical," she pointed out as they entered the dwelling. "Nicholas maintains absolute control over the land, which benefits all of us."

"So he's an environmentalist."

"He's many things, Thomas."

"So I've heard."

She nodded, caution filtering into her when she noticed the speculation on his face.

"I have the distinct impression that you, Benteen, and several others have a very complicated shared history."

"Does it matter?"

"My gut tells me it does."

Geneva abruptly closed the front door. It slammed shut like a punctuation mark on the past.

Thomas stopped her from taking more than a few steps into the foyer. He placed his hand on her shoulder and forced her to turn around.

"Why the secrets, Geneva?"

"Some things don't concern you or anyone else."

"I don't agree."

"You're wrong, so change the subject."

"If I'm wrong, then why are you so upset right now?"

"I'm not upset," she protested. "And I refuse to be badgered by anyone, including you."

"There are a lot of rumors among the local residents about Benteen."

"Gossip."

"That, too," he conceded.

"I don't indulge in either," she said, the emphatic slashing of her hands reinforcing her point.

"It is alleged that he was a mercenary before he took up residence in Cedar Grove," Thomas persisted.

"It is *alleged* that there are little creatures from other planets who visit Earth on a nightly basis."

He ignored her sarcastic response. "The rumor mill indicates that many of the residents of his property are also ex-mercenaries."

"Rumors are, by their very definition, unsubstantiated speculation. Nothing more."

"Why be so evasive?"

"I'm not being evasive. I just don't have anything more to say."

"I suspect that there are a thousand and one things that you'd like to say, because the burden you're carrying is getting very heavy."

Startled by his insight, she stared at him.

"Some people think you and Benteen were lovers. Might even still be, for that matter."

"More unsubstantiated speculation."

Thomas nodded. "I agree."

"You do?"

"You don't have a duplicitous bone in your body. You would have told me by now if you and Nick had been lovers. And if you were now, it would be obvious."

"We're friends. We always will be," she whispered.

"What about allies? Comrades-in-arms?"

Geneva stiffened.

"Talk to me," he pressed, the litigator emerging.

"Don't tell me what to do."

"I'm not. I'm asking you to trust me."

"I do." She actually did, she realized, and it shocked her for a moment.

"It's about time," Thomas said as he moved toward her.

"You're rushing me."

He stopped walking.

"You're also relentless, single-minded, stubborn . . ." She ran out of words.

"A real son of a bitch when I want something," he supplied.

"That, too." She shook her head. "Do you want a tour of this place or not?"

"Lead the way," he signed in response.

She didn't move. "I don't know what to do about you."

He studied her for several silent moments. She shifted uneasily under the force of his penetrating inspection.

Thomas stepped closer, lifted his hand, and stroked her cheek with fingertips. "Don't shut me out. You've been through too much, Geneva Talmadge, and the world is tough to face without a partner. Friends and allies can't fulfill all your needs. I found that out the hard way, and I suspect you have, as well."

"What do you want from me?" she whispered, suddenly terrified that he understood not just the true extent of her reckless hunger for him, but also the depth of her loneliness in recent years.

"What do you want from me?" he countered.

Everything, she realized. Everything, and then some. My God, I must be insane.

His gaze narrowed, as if he'd heard her thoughts.

"Please don't do this to me," she said.

"Don't do what? Don't care about you? Don't feel? Don't want you? Don't make it clear that there's a fire inside me because of you? Don't do what, Geneva?"

"Don't invade my life and turn it upside down on some kind of a lark. I wouldn't survive it if you did that to me. I'm not like the women you've known."

"Thank God for small favors," he muttered.

"What?" she signed because he'd failed to.

"I'm relieved that you are different."

She squared her shoulders and lifted her chin. "I will not be used."

"You know in your heart that that isn't my intention."

She felt herself weakening, felt herself giving in. She prayed that he'd just spoken the truth, because much more than her heart was at stake. Lives could be jeopardized if she made an error in judgment.

"What are you thinking right now?" he asked.

"I want to believe you," she admitted. As she stood there, Geneva cursed fate for the secrets she felt compelled to keep out of love, loyalty, and self-preservation.

"You can, but I guess I'll have to keep proving it to you, won't I?"

"That may not be possible."

"I'll make it possible," he vowed.

Geneva didn't say anything else. What could she say? Turning away, she walked the length of the foyer and entered the living room.

Thomas followed her.

Despite the fact that she wanted to flee, Geneva remained. She transformed herself into the ultimate real estate agent, describing in detail every aspect of the spacious dwelling as they made their way from room to room.

All the while she corralled her emotions. Although he clearly saw through her ploy, Geneva felt grateful that Thomas seemed willing to cooperate. She couldn't help wondering how long this reprieve would last, and how much longer she could conceal the truth about her past.

FIVE

Thomas refrained from questioning her any further. He wanted her too much now to risk alienating her. Until Geneva Talmadge, he'd never met a woman he couldn't walk away from without a moment's regret.

A part of him resented his response to her, while some instinct that grew stronger each day assured him that he would never know any real happiness without her. Having reached the age of forty relatively unscathed by affairs of the heart, he knew in his gut that he'd finally met his destiny.

Thomas also sensed the futility of questioning Geneva about her friends. Close-mouthed and stubborn enough to stand her ground, she obviously trusted very few people. That reality gnawed on his nerves and his pride, but he kept his frustration under wraps.

It would be easy enough for him to use his far-reaching professional resources to investigate her past. But although biding his time frustrated him, he wanted her to discover that she could confide in him without the risk of betrayal.

He didn't intend to give up on Geneva. He couldn't. He wanted this woman in his life, and he promised himself that he would do everything in his power to convince her that she wasn't some conquest he'd set his sights on.

Thomas respected her loyalty to Benteen and her other friends, even envied it, but whether or not she realized it, Geneva reinforced the rumors he'd heard with her wary behavior and secretive attitude. He had a tough time, though, imagining her in the role of a mercenary. He suspected that she'd lived on its fringes, probably as someone's lover or as a relative of someone once closely associated with Benteen and his people.

"Thomas?"

He glanced at her, the sound of her low voice finally penetrating his thoughts. "Yes?"

"You're a million miles away."

He shrugged, summoning a smile as he met her curious gaze. "I haven't missed the high points."

"I hope not. Why don't we go back down to the kitchen? There's a survey map in the pantry that shows the boundary lines of the acreage that's also for sale. Shall we take a look at it?" she signed.

He nodded. "Good idea."

He followed Geneva as she led the way down the rear staircase, across the hallway, and into the spacious kitchen at the rear of the house.

She pulled open the double doors to the pantry. Once she found the map, she spread it across the kitchen counter for his inspection.

Thomas stood beside her, the subtle fragrance she wore teasing his senses.

She signed and spoke as she faced him. "As you can see, the property encompasses areas that have been designated as wildlife refuges. Nicholas will probably include a clause in any sales contract which will guarantee that those areas will remain undeveloped. The state of Nevada is also very protective of the refuges, especially the eagle sanctuary, and they'll expect ironclad guarantees from you before they'll sign off on the sale."

"Nick briefed me on the situation." Thomas stepped back after inspecting the property lines on the map. "I'm prepared to make an offer on the lodge and the acreage today." He then named a dollar figure.

Her surprise at the amount showed in her startled expression. "I'll convey your offer to Nicholas as soon as possible."

Thomas resisted her attempt to delay the

process. "He led me to believe that you're empowered to act on his behalf. Is my offer too low?"

"I am empowered, and I suspect you already know that your offer is quite appropriate, but the lodge is in a remote area. Being so isolated might not appeal to you after a few months. A trial run makes more sense, especially since you've spent the last several years of your life in the city. I think Nicholas would suggest a lease, with the option to purchase the property at the end of either six or twelve months. That way you'll have a chance to experience the winter months before you make a permanent commitment."

"It's November," he pointed out. "And I haven't forgotten what it means to be snowed in."

Geneva persisted. "I believe it would be best if we try a lease with an option to buy."

Although frustrated with her delaying tactics, he managed not to lose his temper, but he decided not to avoid the real issue at hand. "You don't want me as your nearest neighbor, do you?"

"It isn't that, it's just that I—"

He reached out and touched her cheek.

Geneva fell silent, her eyes locked on his face.

Thomas felt the stillness that settled over

her, felt the arousal that steamed through his veins. "You're holding your breath. Why?"

Geneva inhaled sharply, then took one step away.

He moved closer. "I want you, but I'd never force you to do anything that felt wrong to you."

She stiffened and stared at him.

"You don't have to be afraid of me, Geneva. I'm not a threat, nor am I a fool. I realize you have some genuine concerns about my motives."

"I don't know you that well yet."

"I think you do."

"I don't," she insisted.

He weighed his next comment carefully. "If you know yourself, then you know some very important facts about me."

Her slender hands moved like lightning. "I don't understand what you mean."

"You will in time. Look, you know I want you. You knew that the first time we talked."

"You're talking about sex. I'm not so irresponsible that I'll sleep with a man just because he wants me."

He didn't let himself react to her flaring temper. "I admit that making love is a part of the equation, but it's just part of it. I'm not asking you to be irresponsible, but I think you want me just as much as I want you. Why deny it?"

Spots of color flagged her cheeks. "Life isn't that simple. Not my life, anyway."

"You're right. Real life can be like a minefield at times."

"We shouldn't be having this conversation. It's pointless."

"I don't agree," he said.

"Thomas, you don't understand."

"Then help me to understand."

She gathered herself then, and an implacable expression filled her face. "We're here to discuss the lodge, nothing else."

Thomas ignored her comment. "What do your instincts tell you about me, Geneva?"

She hesitated, studying him so intently that he wondered if she'd bother to answer him. When she did respond, she surprised him.

"My instincts tell me that you're the first man I've ever met who makes me want to abandon my common sense. My instincts keep urging me to go with the moment every time you get near me or if you touch me. But other instincts, the ones that have kept me sane and safe for several years now, tell me to watch my step with you."

"That's honest," he said.

"I'm always honest," she said emphatically. "With myself and with those people who are a part of my life."

"Does the latter category include me?"

She hesitated, then nodded very reluctantly. "It does now, even though I doubt the wisdom of it. I won't be used."

"I meant it before when I said I wouldn't rush you or try to use you. I care about you."

"I care about you, too. Because I care, I'm asking you to accept the lease. It's the logical thing to do."

He grudgingly smiled. "You drive a hard bargain."

"Not really. I'm just trying to be practical. Spending close to a million dollars on a home and property is a major step. I don't want you to regret it, especially since I'm not included in the transaction. Whatever happens, or doesn't happen, between us has to remain a separate issue."

His smile broadened. He liked her bluntness, even found it refreshing and in sharp contrast to the innuendo that most people indulged in. He especially appreciated her ability to hold her own.

"Regret won't ever be an issue for me, Geneva. I'm here to stay."

"If your law practice isn't a success, you might not want to remain in Cedar Grove."

"I'm not leaving, Geneva," he said, his voice as hard as stone.

She nodded but only after searching his face, clearly taking the time to judge for herself the truth of his statement. Turning to the map still spread out on the countertop, she rolled it into a snug cylinder.

Thomas placed his hand on her shoulder.

Geneva glanced his way, her expression neutral.

"Cedar Grove is my home now. I'm not going back to life in the fast lane. I've had enough of it and the people who populate it." He hesitated. "I can't do it anymore."

She frowned. "You have regrets about your past, don't you?"

A muscle ticked in his jaw, but he answered her. "I have a lot of regrets, but I don't plan on having any more."

He recalled his last case. He'd successfully thwarted a potentially crippling lawsuit against a car manufacturer following a series of auto-related deaths. The faces of the victims' families still haunted him. Their lives had been shattered by devastating loss, and he'd compounded their anguish by making certain that they received no just compensation. He knew he would live with his regret over the outcome of the case for the rest of his life.

Geneva reached out to him. Her fingertips grazed the tops of his knuckles, startling him from his memories. He met her gaze and glimpsed her concern.

"Are you all right?" she asked.

Unaware of the sadness etched into his

hard-featured face, he jerked a nod in her direction. "I'm fine."

"I shouldn't have pried. I apologize."

"You didn't pry. Someday, I'll tell you about it. I need a home first, and I need to feel rooted again. It's been a long time since I've felt as though I belonged someplace."

Her expression softened, and a sad smile graced her lips. "I understand about belonging. Until I moved to Cedar Grove, I never felt as though I was a part of anything even vaguely normal."

He chuckled, but there was little humor in the sound. "I think we have more in common than you realize."

She absently nodded as she studied him. "Perhaps we do."

He withstood her inspection, feeling for the first time in his life that he didn't need to hide the emptiness he often felt. He knew she understood isolation and loneliness, especially the kind that happens even when a person is surrounded by friends and coworkers. He needed her compassion. He needed her touch, not just because she aroused him, but because there was a gentleness in her that spoke to his soul.

He needed *her*.

Geneva managed a half smile. "I think we should draw up the appropriate documents, don't you?"

"If you'll compromise."

She inclined her head. "In what way?"

"A three-month lease, with the understanding that my offer takes precedence over any others of equal or lesser value. The ceiling on the asking price will never exceed ten percent of my current offer. I also expect to be given thirty days at the end of the lease in which to execute or withdraw from the purchase option."

"I believe Nicholas would accept your terms, although he might feel inclined to debate them because he enjoys negotiating. I personally don't see any point in doing that, though."

Thomas relaxed. "Then let's take care of the necessary paperwork."

"All right."

They walked to the front door. Thomas knew that their relationship had shifted onto new ground. He also sensed that Geneva, who seemed subdued but less wary, felt the change between them.

She paused in the entryway to put on her leather gloves.

Thomas asked, "Do you want to stop by your place before I drive you into town to pick up your Jeep?"

She nodded. "Please. I need to get my briefcase."

"We can take care of the lease agreement this afternoon."

"Sounds good, but I'll need to confirm everything with Nicholas."

"I don't have a problem with that."

She fell silent, briefly studying the planked floor of the entry hall before lifting her face. "I . . . I really don't mind that we'll be neighbors."

Thomas smiled. "I don't mind, either. In fact, I'm looking forward to it." He reached for the doorknob, then hesitated. His smile faded as he cast an intent look in her direction.

"Have we forgotten something?" Geneva asked.

He exhaled, the sound ragged in the silence as he turned toward her. "Just one thing."

"What?"

"I need to hold you."

Her eyes widened, but she didn't speak or sign a response at first. She simply looked at him for several moments, then startled him when she said, "I'd like that very much, Thomas."

She walked into his arms a heartbeat later.

Shocked, he gathered her to him without hesitation, unwilling to question the impulse that had prompted his admission or the one that had guided her to him. He merely pressed her against him, cherishing the feel of her, wondering what it would be like to join his body to hers, to bury himself within her. At the images that filled his mind, his embrace tightened and heat surged into his groin.

She trembled against him, but she didn't draw back. He felt her uncertainty and her restraint, and even though he knew that she wanted him, it still seemed like an eternity before he felt her arms slide around his waist.

Relieved, Thomas exhaled. As much as he desired Geneva, he reminded himself that he couldn't risk overwhelming her. He fought yet again for control over his body.

She rested her forehead against his shoulder, slowly relaxing, slowly releasing the tension evidenced in the quick, shallow breaths she took.

Thomas lowered his head and pressed his lips against the side of her neck. Her skin reminded him of satin—warm, fragrant satin. He surrendered to the intoxicating scent of her.

She shifted forward, her full breasts plumping against his chest, her hands sweeping up his broad back. He groaned, pure instinct driving him as he cupped her hips with his hands and guided her closer. His loins already ached painfully, but he tortured himself nonetheless by rubbing his maleness against her.

Geneva sucked in a breath, then lifted her head from his shoulder. She opened her mouth to speak, then closed it, as if too bewildered to say anything.

Thomas met her gaze. He saw the desire that glazed her eyes, felt it in the shaking of her slender body. "Talk to me," he invited, speaking slowly so that she could read his lips, because he didn't want to take his hands from her.

"I don't know what to say."

He signed, "What are you feeling right now?"

Lifting her hands, she answered, "Too much. Much more than I expected."

"I know what you mean."

"Losing control scares me," she admitted.

"What about loving? Does that scare you, as well?"

She paled. "Yes."

"Me, too."

"You're being very honest."

"I can't be anything else with you. There's too much at risk to lie to you."

"I know," she said, still looking at him with an expression of mingling shock, curiosity, and the barest hint of invitation. Her tongue darted out to moisten her lower lip.

Thomas felt his restraint shatter. Slowly lowering his head, he sought her lips. He tasted the surprise and relief that rushed out of her in the exhalation that came from deep inside her body. He tasted and savored, indulging himself by tracing the shape of her lips with the tip of his tongue, then gently teething her lower lip until she moaned softly.

She edged even closer, angling her head when he released her from the tender vise. She parted her lips.

Another invitation, Thomas realized. His heart raced, the muscles in his body thrummed with tension, and desire scorched his bloodstream.

He kissed her then with the kind of tenderness that he'd never associated with himself, kissed her with a gentleness akin to worship. He felt her hands smooth up his back beneath his jacket, then felt her fingertips drift down as she traced the shallow indentation of his spine.

He longed to strip away the clothes that covered both of them. He knew better, though. But as if to reward his patience, Geneva tugged his sweater free from the waistband of his jeans and rhythmically kneaded his lower back with her fingertips. The soft leather gloves covering her fingers added an extra dimension of sensation to her caress.

Thomas shuddered, then plunged his tongue deeply into her mouth as he simultaneously lifted her, then wrapped her legs around his hips.

Geneva gasped, then darted her tongue into his mouth, searching, stroking, tantalizing, searing his senses in the intimate duel that followed.

He welcomed the sudden change in her response, welcomed this signal that she returned his desire. Without releasing her mouth, he moved toward the staircase and sank down on one of the lower steps. He relieved Geneva of her parka, then shed his own heavy jacket. Still perched astride his thighs, she tore off her gloves and cast them aside. She smoothed her hands up over his chest, and combed her fingers through his dark hair.

Geneva trembled violently when Thomas placed his hands over her breasts. She arched into his palms, little moans carried on breathless pants that spilled past her lips as he shaped and molded her flesh with his fingers. His name spilled out of her.

He needed to feel the heat of her skin, so he unbuttoned the bodice of her jumpsuit. Naked beneath the fabric, her erect nipples stabbed at his palms, as if begging for his mouth. He lifted her then, despite her groan of protest when their lips parted, and brought her breasts level with his mouth.

Cupping her breast, he drew the taut nipple into his mouth and teethed her sensitive flesh. She groaned, the sound so seductive that Thomas wanted to plunge into her then. Instead, he slid his free hand between her parted thighs, cupping her, then stroking her until she surged against the pressure of the heel of his hand. He stroked her with a steadily escalating rhythm that matched the pull of his lips at her breast. Her repeated gasps of pleasure were an erotic entreaty, one that he was powerless to ignore.

Geneva was more sexually volatile than he'd ever imagined she might be, and the prospect of experiencing the full impact of her sensuality almost made him explode. But he kept his focus on her, wanting to pleasure her until she succumbed totally to the release he intended to give her.

Taking wasn't an issue for him now, even though he wanted Geneva more than he'd ever wanted any other woman in his entire life. Giving meant more. Far more, but he didn't pause to ask himself why.

She called out his name, her hands frantic as she clutched at his shoulders. He intensified the pressure of his hand and suckled her more forcefully. Then a groan tore through her a few moments later. She stiffened, and then cried out as waves of sensation buffeted her body.

When Geneva finally crumpled into his arms, Thomas gathered her close and marveled over the stunning force of her climax. He'd never known a more responsive woman.

As he held her, Thomas felt the aftershocks that made her body quiver, then the tears that wet his lips when he leaned down to kiss her cheek.

Turning away from his gaze, Geneva covered her face with her hands.

Thomas refused to allow her to hide from him. He tugged her hands away, then cupped her head between his palms and forced her to look at him.

Geneva glanced away, struggled briefly, then suddenly gave up the fight. She met his gaze.

"Don't be embarrassed. Please," he said, speaking slowly.

She stared at him, her blue eyes huge in her pale face. "I'm not."

"Then what's wrong? Why are you crying?"

She wiped away the tears on her cheeks before answering him. "I felt . . . I didn't know . . ." She stopped, clearly frustrated.

It can't be, Thomas thought, but he suspected he knew what troubled her. Her startled reaction to his touch had been more telling than she probably realized. "Was that your first climax with a partner?" he asked.

Flushing, she nodded.

"The men you've known were idiots."

Geneva held up a single finger. "One man. A long time ago."

"Then *he* was an idiot."

She smiled faintly. "Selfish. Not like you." Her smile faded. She deliberately shifted against him, then her hand drifted down between their bodies and she smoothed her fingertips over the ample evidence of his unappeased desire.

Thomas smothered a groan, still so aroused that his body throbbed for release.

"Not very fair to you," she said.

Thomas chuckled in spite of his physical discomfort. "I'll be all right. I told you I wouldn't rush you. I meant it."

"Most men wouldn't care. They would expect . . ."

He captured one of her hands and pressed a kiss to each fingertip. "I care, and I can wait until you're ready. You're worth waiting for, Geneva."

She leaned forward, claimed his lips tenderly, and kissed him. Once she eased back from him, she signed, "I can't promise when. I can only be myself and trust my instincts."

Because he valued her honesty, Thomas nodded soberly. "No expectations, no disappointments."

"Thank you for understanding."

"I do," he said. "Far more than I think you even realize."

He held her then, savoring the bond they'd forged. A little while later, he helped her rearrange her clothing before they departed the lodge.

Following a stop at Geneva's chalet, Thomas drove her to the garage in Cedar Grove to collect her Jeep. He then followed her to the business district of the small northern Nevada town. Before the close of business that day Thomas signed the documents to lease the lodge. He also telephoned his moving company and ordered the delivery of his household goods, which had been in storage since his departure from San Diego the previous month.

SIX

Although it surprised her to realize it, Geneva truly wasn't embarrassed by what had transpired at the lodge, especially after she replayed the entire episode through her mind several times in the days that followed. At first, she feared that she'd made a complete fool of herself, but her anxiety ceased once she settled down enough to think clearly.

The real test came each time she encountered Thomas, either when he stopped into her shop for a few moments of conversation, when they ran into each other in the office building hallways, or when they dined together after work. True to his word, he didn't rush her. His desire for her showed in his eyes, so she appreciated even more his restraint as she embraced the idea of living a less-guarded life.

Even Rose noticed his subdued demeanor, but she credited her nephew's behavior to the pressure of setting up his law office and settling into a new home. Geneva didn't correct her.

The awkwardness Geneva *didn't* feel around Thomas made her briefly wonder if her pride was blinding her to what any other woman might consider a lapse in judgment, but she finally concluded that she could trust the emotions that had guided her into his embrace. At thirty-seven she possessed more than a rudimentary knowledge of human nature. She'd seen people at their best and at their worst, and at many points in between.

Geneva sensed that she might be overanalyzing, but she felt the need to come to terms with her attraction to a man like Thomas Coltrane. A unique man. A man of integrity and honor and strength. A man capable of reawakening her passion and stirring her emotions. The kind of man she'd dreamed of having as a life partner. The same man who was gently, but doggedly, courting her.

Her lack of sexual experience was a reality she knew she couldn't ignore, but she also remembered what her father had told her as a teenager during her first crush. He'd assured her that she would eventually discover that intimacy between two consenting adults transcended any real or imaginary obstacle.

He'd told her that physical desire was nothing to be ashamed or afraid of. And among the people she thought of as her family, she'd witnessed every possible pairing of men and women, from long-term relationships to short-lived affairs.

As she stared at the flames dancing above the logs in the fireplace in her bedroom late one night, she wondered what her father would have said if he'd known that a man like Thomas Coltrane would become the force destined to reacquaint her with her passionate side. She suspected that Patrick would have encouraged the relationship, given it his blessing.

Geneva already knew that she couldn't deny the chemistry between her and Thomas. It literally took her breath away each time she saw him.

Even now her body quickened deep inside at the prospect of making love with him. His touch was the closest thing to heaven. She'd felt his heartbeat in his fingertips when he stroked her body, and she shivered at the thought of experiencing his seductive touch again.

Physical desire wasn't the only thing that drew her to him. He had allowed her a glimpse into his soul, an act of faith that she didn't doubt was a rare occurrence. And what she saw was that Thomas Coltrane understood regret and loneliness. Rather than discourage her, the knowledge served to seduce both her emotions and her heart even more.

Perhaps, she mused, he was the kind of man capable of understanding her past. Perhaps he wouldn't feel compelled to judge her. Perhaps he was the answer to her yearning for the ultimate emotional and physical union between a man and a woman. She knew he felt the same yearning, one he'd managed to contain and control. Because of her. For her.

She exhaled softly as she settled against the pillows on her bed and drew up the quilt. She wanted Thomas, not just as a lover but as a friend, companion, and confidant. She wanted him in her life and in her bed, but did she possess the courage to tell him the truth about herself at the risk of repulsing him?

She realized then that the greatest danger she faced was the possibility of falling in love with him. A voice in her head warned that the point was moot. Geneva didn't bother to contradict it. She already cared about Thomas, cared more deeply than she'd ever cared before.

As she turned off the lamp on the bedside table, she reminded herself that cowardice didn't suit her. The bottom line was simple. She wanted Thomas Coltrane enough to risk her heart. The one thing she refused to risk, however, was the safety of her family. So she had to find a way not to jeopardize those she valued and still satisfy her longing for Thomas.

She drifted off to sleep, wondering how one turned fantasy into reality.

A few days later Geneva was awkwardly juggling the fresh boughs she'd just cut from an ancient pine tree not far from her chalet, when she saw Thomas stroll into the clearing. A welcoming smile sprang to her lips.

He waved and walked toward her. "Rose told me you decided to take the day off," he signed as he spoke.

She met him halfway. "You're a nice surprise."

"When you didn't answer your front door, I thought I'd scout around a bit. I followed the sled tracks."

She deposited the boughs on top of the tall stack already on the sled, then stepped back to dust the needles from her parka.

"It's almost dark. How about some help?"

She glanced up at the early evening sky and shook her head. "I lost track of the time, I'm afraid." Geneva gestured to the boughs. "As you can see, I also overestimated the capacity of my sled."

"No problem." Thomas took an armful of boughs and placed them in her outstretched arms. "If you can handle these, I'll deal with the sled."

"Excellent plan."

He paused, then signed, "You have the sexiest voice."

Startled, she said, "Excuse me?"

He gave her an amused look. "You understood me correctly."

"You're right, I did. You surprised me, that's all."

"Then we're even, Ms. Talmadge, because you've been a constant surprise since the first moment I saw you."

"Is that good or bad?" Geneva teased, responding to his upbeat mood.

"I'm not complaining, so I guess it's good."

She grinned. "I'll have to trust you. In the meantime, my toes are in danger of turning into ice cubes."

He cupped the side of her face with his glove-covered hand. He didn't say anything. He simply studied her upturned face.

Geneva's grin slipped, then faded completely. Desire sparked throughout her body like tiny flash fires. All because of Thomas. All because he'd touched her cheek.

"Is something wrong?" she finally asked.

Thomas withdrew his hand. "Not touching you for more than a week has been hell, but now that I have, everything feels right again."

Amazed by his statement, she whispered, "I'm glad."

"I feel good when I'm around you."

"You've been a stranger to happiness in recent years, haven't you?"

He nodded. Then, although he didn't seem put off by her observation, he changed the subject. "I gather you're about to start making wreaths."

"For the shop. I love the scent of the pine needles. So do my customers. I'm also giving some serious thought to adding decorated wreaths to our winter catalog next year, but it means hiring more staff."

"Might be worth it," Thomas commented.

In companionable silence they made their way along the quarter-mile pathway to the potting shed. Geneva couldn't help but think that she'd never before shared even the simplest pleasures or tasks with a man she loved. She stood on the brink of change. And she welcomed it, just as she wanted to welcome Thomas into her life.

After the boughs were deposited in the potting shed and they had taken off their winter gear, Geneva led the way into the kitchen. She filled two mugs with hot mulled cider, added dashes of cinnamon, and then preceded Thomas into the living room.

"How about a fire?" he asked.

"Please," she murmured. "Matches are on the mantel."

She settled onto the couch that faced the fireplace, sipping cider as Thomas lit the logs. Geneva didn't deny herself the pleasure of watching him. Tall and leanly muscled, he moved with a fluid masculine grace that delighted her senses. She recalled Rose telling her that he'd been an accomplished athlete all through school.

She understood why as her gaze moved up his powerful legs to narrow hips encased in age-softened denim, past his flat belly, which she suspected was ridged with muscles, and onto his wide shoulders. She remembered clinging to those shoulders as her body had splintered apart in the throes of a mind-shattering climax, just as she remembered the strength of his embrace and the way her nipples had tightened to aching points of need as he'd held her close. They puckered tightly now at the thought of his mouth fastened to the sensitive tips, his tongue swirling, his teeth gently scraping over her skin.

Geneva shivered with arousal. The cider in her mug sloshed. Grabbing her napkin, she dried her fingers.

When she lifted her gaze to his face, she realized by his expression that Thomas understood the journey her thoughts had just taken.

She felt foolish until she noticed the condition of his lower body.

She noticed, too, the tightening of his jaw and the darkening of his eyes. She held her breath for a long while as she was swamped by emotions she suddenly couldn't control, emotions like hope and uncertainty, desire and anxiety, and love. She suddenly loathed her lack of experience, but a moment later it occurred to her that Thomas was the kind of man who would teach her whatever she wanted to learn.

He sank into a wing chair directly across from her. The intensity of his gaze prompted Geneva to fill in the silence between them.

"How's the unpacking coming along?" she asked, then hated the fact that she'd revealed her nervousness by asking such a dumb question.

"It's almost done, thanks to Rose. She's been great."

"She's a wonderful woman. I've never known anyone like her." Geneva fell silent. She couldn't think of anything to say that wasn't inane.

"When I saw you the day before yesterday, you were exhausted. You look more rested now."

"I was tired, but not any longer. This is our busy season, so my schedule's pretty demanding. Late spring and the summer months are a restful time, though." Geneva smiled. "Playing hooky agrees with me, although it's a bit self-indulgent."

"I missed seeing you there today."

"But you see me almost every day."

"During the workday, and we're both usually on the run." He gave her a meaningful look. "It's not enough, Geneva. Not nearly enough."

Geneva felt the same way. Setting aside her mug, she got to her feet and approached the fireplace. She moved the screen into position as the flames licked the sides of the logs.

Squaring her shoulders, she turned to face Thomas. "You promised you wouldn't rush me," she reminded him.

"I haven't."

"No, you haven't, and I've appreciated it."

"It's been damn tough, but I knew it was what you needed." He studied her for several silent seconds. "You haven't said anything about what happened between us at the lodge."

"What do you want me to say?"

He looked momentarily surprised by her question. "I'd like to know how you feel."

"I've thought about it a lot," she admitted.

"So have I."

"You surprised me. And I surprised myself."

"I still want you, but even more now."

Her pulse raced. She fought for control, fought the urge to take his hand and lead him up the stairs to her bedroom. It was too soon, and she knew it. "I don't have any regrets about what happened between us, Thomas."

"None?"

"None whatsoever. We're obviously attracted to each other."

"There's more going on here than a sexual attraction."

"You're right."

"You've tried to analyze it, though, haven't you?"

His insight didn't surprise her. Thomas Coltrane didn't miss much, which made him a mixed blessing. "I have to confess that I've been accused by my friends of overthinking most situations."

"Where do we go from here?"

She smiled suddenly. "My experience is pretty limited."

He laughed. "And mine isn't?"

Geneva shrugged. "If the shoe fits . . ."

He grimaced. "You're waiting for me to make the next move."

"I kind of thought that you were. Making moves, I mean. Fortunately, they're little moves, or I would have gone into hibernation for the winter."

"I want you every time I see you."

His blunt remark simply heightened the

desire she felt, but she pointed out the obvious. "That's chemistry."

"Wanting you is only a part of the equation."

"What are the other parts?" she asked.

"I like you."

"I like you, too."

"You trust me."

"Instinctively, rather than logically."

"I trust you."

His admission caught her off guard. It also validated something she'd suspected. "You don't usually trust women, do you?"

"I don't think I've ever consciously thought about it."

"Why not?"

"I don't usually let anyone that close anymore."

"You're being very honest with me."

Thomas didn't speak for almost a full minute. Geneva held her breath and waited.

"There's a lot at stake between us," he finally said.

"I know," she whispered. Her thoughts snagged then on her past, the small group of people who populated her insular world, and her dream that she would be accepted for herself.

He shook his head, a rueful smile on his lips. "I'm starting to remember the awkward days of my youth."

She sobered, his reference to his teens a jarring reminder of how unconventional hers had been. "My youth never included conversations like this one."

"Nor mine."

She started to walk back to the couch, but he reached out and captured her hand, halting her. Geneva squeezed his fingers, then slipped free of his hold.

"What did your youth include?" he asked as she resumed her seat on the couch.

She shrugged. "A lot of different things."

"That's illuminating."

She flushed. "Sorry. The evasion was pure reflex."

"A self-protective one, I suspect."

"Maybe." She paused, briefly weighed her options, and forged ahead. "Yes. I'm very self-protective. I'm also protective of my friends."

"You're talking about secrets, aren't you?" Thomas asked.

"To some degree."

He leaned forward, elbows resting on his knees and the palms of his hands pressed together as he pondered her. "I wouldn't ever betray you."

"I think I've finally realized that."

"Then we're making progress. Why don't you tell me about your childhood?" he invited.

"What would you like to know?"

He leaned back in his chair. "Anything that suits you. Your comment a few weeks ago about not living a normal life intrigued me."

She ran her fingertip along the rim of the mug sitting on the lamp table beside the couch. Thomas wasn't prying, she realized. She reminded herself that people got acquainted by sharing information, both past and present, about themselves. His curiosity was normal. She met his gaze, but still she hesitated. She didn't know where or how to begin.

As if sensing her uncertainty, he helped her. "Where were you born, Geneva?"

"In Boston. I spent my early years there, as well."

"An only child?"

"Yes. My mother couldn't have any other children. My father told me that they'd planned to have at least a half dozen."

"You must have had cousins."

"Several. My mother was one of eight children. After my father left, Erin and I moved in with my grandparents."

"Erin?"

She nodded. "My mother. Erin Talmadge. She died when I was twelve."

Thomas frowned. "Erin Talmadge? The concert pianist?"

"Yes."

"She was a legend. An international sensation. Quite a remarkable woman, like her daughter."

Geneva considered the night and day differences between a pianist capable of transporting her audience to the heights of pleasure with her extraordinary talent and an explosives expert who could take down a bridge with a few well-placed charges. There was no comparing the two as far as she was concerned. She'd concluded long ago that her penance for a misspent youth was her deafness. She would never be able to listen to the old recordings of her mother's Carnegie Hall concerts.

"My mother was quite unique. No one will ever be like her, least of all me."

His gaze narrowed. "You're very hard on yourself."

"I'm a realist, Thomas. I've learned to be."

Geneva glanced at the blazing logs in the fireplace, keenly aware of just how disappointed Erin Talmadge would have been had she witnessed her daughter's life.

". . . Patrick your father?"

As she looked again at Thomas, she caught only a part of his question. She frowned. "How did you know his name?"

"I heard that part of your conversation

with Nick when I tripped over you two in the hallway that first day."

"Patrick was my father. He was an engineer . . . and a self-confessed vagabond."

"Is that all he was?"

She exhaled, treading carefully through her memories as she decided which parts to reveal and which to censor. "Patrick dabbled, and he loved what he called grand adventures. He also liked living on the edge."

"And did you live on the edge, too?"

"Yes, but only after my mother died. She didn't approve of Patrick's wanderlust. He traveled the world, went to places most people either dream about or avoid like the proverbial plague. It's why their marriage failed, although I feel certain that Erin died loving him."

"Define living on the edge for me," Thomas urged.

"I'm not sure I can, and I don't want to bore you."

"Try, please."

As she studied him, she reminded herself that she no longer needed to be so guarded or self-protective, but she proceeded with caution nonetheless. "Patrick liked being smack in the middle of chaos. So did his friends. Civil wars in Third World countries, governments being overthrown, invasions, that sort of thing." She took a steadying breath, then continued. "When Erin died and he showed up at her funeral, I hadn't seen him in nearly five years. I was almost thirteen then, and you can probably imagine how fascinating he was to me, especially given my sheltered life. When Patrick asked me if I wanted to travel the world with him, I jumped at the chance over my grandparents' objections. I packed a suitcase and off we went to explore the world. I had no comprehension of what life with Patrick would entail. It was something of a shock."

"And exciting?"

She smiled, but her expression grew contemplative after a few moments. She again shifted her gaze to the fireplace. "Exciting, terrifying, exotic, and dangerous. I was isolated from people my own age, especially when I was in my teens. Once I was a little bit more mature, I adapted quite well. I inherited his friends, and they became my family. I can also live out of a single suitcase for months at a time better than anyone I know."

Her attempt at humor fell flat, and she knew it the instant the words spilled past her lips. She cringed inwardly.

"You told me he was an engineer," Thomas said. "Is that how he supported you both?"

Geneva nodded warily. "In a manner of speaking."

Thomas said nothing. He simply looked at her.

Geneva supplied what she knew he was waiting to hear—the truth. "Patrick was a munitions and explosives specialist."

Surprise flared in his eyes. "He made bombs?"

"Yes. He had quite a reputation in the international community."

"He knew Benteen, didn't he?"

"Quite well." Geneva felt so tense now that she feared she might shatter into a thousand pieces if Thomas reacted badly to what she'd just told him.

When he said nothing in the minutes that followed, she got to her feet and walked out of the living room. Her hands shook as she stood at the kitchen stove and refilled her mug.

Geneva told herself that she possessed the strength to survive his departure. And that's what she expected—that he would leave. After all, Thomas was an intelligent man and more than capable of reading between the lines, and she'd just told him that she was the daughter of a mercenary.

Taking a deep breath, Geneva turned away from the stove, and saw Thomas standing in the doorway of the kitchen. She controlled the anxiety raging within by sheer force of will as she watched him make his way across the room.

How in the world could she tell him that she'd learned her father's skill with explosives? And how could she tell him that she hadn't been just an observer, but an active participant in that underworld of violence and destruction? What man would want a woman capable of such things?

She raised her chin. He paused in front of her, relieved her of the mug she gripped with both hands, and then drew her into his arms.

She shook like a willow battered by a hard wind as he held her and stroked her back with his hands. Several moments passed, moments during which she struggled to comprehend his intentions and his reaction to what she'd revealed.

Thomas released her and stepped back. "I don't understand all the implications of what you've just told me, but the one thing I can't get past right now is my gut instinct that you somehow feel responsible for the choices your parents made."

She shook her head, denial instantaneous. "That's not true."

"Don't lie to me. There's no need," Thomas insisted.

Geneva insisted, "I am responsible for myself and no one else!"

Thomas gave her a speculative look. "Then why are you so upset right now?"

She hedged, too upset and ashamed to do

anything else. "I don't like discussing the past. It bothers me."

"That's not an answer, Geneva."

"It's the only answer I'm willing to provide at the moment," she countered, her defenses lined up around her like sentries.

His gaze narrowed as he studied her. "What are you afraid of?"

Her belligerence evaporated. "Myself," she whispered hollowly.

"What do you mean?" he asked, clearly confused.

"I don't know." Her hands fell to her sides. She walked away from him.

Thomas followed her and forced her to turn around and look at him. "Don't push me away. Help me to understand what's going on inside your head right now."

"I can't. I thought I could, but I can't. I'm sorry."

"Geneva, this is crazy. Talk to me."

Anger and frustration swamped her. "Don't do this to me!" she cried. "You don't want to know the truth, Thomas."

His lawyerly calm absent, he shouted, "I want you, dammit! I want all of you. The good, the bad, the happiness, and the pain. Everything. Why won't you believe me?"

She desperately wanted to believe him, but she feared the heartbreak that would follow if

he decided that he'd made an error in judgment. "Please leave, Thomas." Tears filled her
eyes as she said the words. And they spilled
down her cheeks as she watched him honor
her request.

SEVEN

Thomas gave himself an entire day to calm down before he considered his next move with Geneva. He then gave her an additional seventy-two hours to regroup before he showed up unannounced at her home.

He spotted her at the living room window when he pulled into the circular driveway in front of the chalet. Making his way to the front door, he waited for her to respond to his presence. He knew that she might decide to ignore him. He hoped she wouldn't, but he reminded himself, not for the first time, that she was the most stubborn woman he'd ever met.

Geneva pulled open the door, her expression guarded as she looked up at him. Clad in a heavy sweater, jeans, and fluffy slippers, and with her golden hair flowing across her shoulders and down her back, she looked more like a coed than a successful businesswoman.

"Peace offering," Thomas carefully finger-spelled, displaying both his effort to supplement his signing ability and a vintage bottle of wine for her inspection.

Her eyes flared wide with surprise at his finger spelling attempt, but she didn't say anything for a moment. She watched the plump snowflakes that swirled around him as he stood there. Some of the damp flakes clung to his hair and clothing, and the crisp, below-zero temperature gave his face a ruddy look.

"I wasn't expecting you," she finally signed.

And I sure as hell wasn't expecting you, Geneva Talmadge, he thought, *but now that I've found you, I'm not leaving.*

"This isn't a good time, Thomas," she said. "Perhaps you should—"

"Will there ever be a good time?" he asked.

She started to respond, seemed to reconsider, and then simply stepped aside and motioned him indoors with an elegant sweep of her hand.

Thomas silently thanked the impulse that prompted her grudging hospitality. After handing her the wine bottle, he shed his heavy jacket and boots.

Geneva remained silent as she led the way

to the kitchen. Her silence persisted as she placed the wine bottle on the countertop. Once she located a cork remover and two long-stemmed goblets for the wine, she stepped back.

Thomas felt her wary gaze as he uncorked the white wine and poured it. He congratulated himself on his restraint, because all he really wanted to do was draw her into his arms and indulge himself with the taste and fragrance of this woman. Instead, he handed her a half-filled wineglass, followed her to the table in the nook adjacent to the kitchen, and settled into a chair opposite her.

"How are you?" she signed.

Polite conversation. It's a start, he reminded himself. "Busy with work. Like you, I imagine."

She nodded, then took a sip of wine. "This is very nice."

"I'm a partner in the winery. This particular blend is one of my favorites."

"Are you hungry? I can fix you a sandwich or a bowl of soup."

"Not necessary. I've already had supper. Rose is single-handedly making up for all the years I've been away."

"She's happy to have you home, and she enjoys spoiling the people she loves."

"I've picked up a few pounds, courtesy of her home cooking."

"I had the same problem when we first became friends."

Thomas relaxed a little. "How'd you solve it?"

"Simple. I took smaller portions." She smiled.

"Sneaky," he said with an answering grin.

"Smart," she countered. "I didn't want to have to buy a whole new wardrobe."

A sudden movement drew his attention. Thomas shifted his gaze to the view of the backyard visible from the wall of glass behind Geneva. A family of foxes, each one seemingly oblivious to the motion sensors that sent bright light spilling across the landscape, cavorted around the base of a snow-dusted tree stump.

As he watched them, Thomas reflected on how much he'd missed Geneva in recent days. The absence of her smile had begun to remind him of an absent sun on a summer day.

"Those little guys visit almost every night," she remarked after noticing the activity that had drawn his gaze. "They're like the Three Stooges."

Thomas chuckled as he looked back at her. "I'd forgotten sights like that. I'd forgotten a lot of things, I guess." He shoved his fingers through his hair.

"You seem a bit distracted tonight," she said.

"Maybe a little," he conceded. "I've spent most of the day wrestling with how to handle a new case."

"You have more than one client now. That's wonderful."

"I have a half-dozen clients," he told her, signing effortlessly.

Geneva briefly pondered his announcement. "You've become very proficient at signing in recent weeks."

"I'm highly motivated."

Glancing away, she absently smoothed a single fingertip up and down the stem of her wineglass.

Thomas waited for her to look at him before speaking. "It's important to me to be able to communicate with you, Geneva. If I hadn't known how to sign because of my mother, I would have enrolled in a class."

She sank back in her chair. "I don't know that you should bother."

"You're worth the effort, or don't you agree?"

"Thank you," she answered, not really answering him and looking a little dazed by his bluntness. "I'm glad about your clients Thomas. It appears that you'll be able to eat this winter."

He chuckled. He knew that even without his clients he could afford to feed himself and everyone else in Cedar Grove for the next hundred years. "So it seems."

"Are they challenging? The cases, I mean."

"More than I expected them to be, but I'm on the opposite side of the legal fence these days, and it takes some getting used to."

"I don't understand. It seems logical to assume that you'd be able to anticipate the tactics of your adversaries, so you'll have an edge in court."

"I don't doubt my abilities. It's the people. I'm representing real people for a change."

"I assumed you always had."

"Not really. This feels more . . ." He paused, searching for the right word.

"Personal?" Geneva finger-spelled.

Thomas nodded, pleased that she understood. He remembered the manner in which his parents had often completed each other's sentences and thoughts. He'd never experienced that degree of closeness with a woman, not even his ex-wife. It was then that he realized being with Geneva was his only hope of ever finding the inner peace he'd searched for in vain during the last several years. Without her, his decision to make a new start would end up a hollow victory.

"Very personal," Thomas answered, careful not to betray his thoughts, "and far more important. This is the kind of law my father practiced. It's the kind of law I'd originally planned to practice."

"You are now," she reminded him.

"Better late than never," he quipped, his voice harsh to his own ears. He wondered if he'd ever get beyond his conviction that he'd wasted far too many years on meaningless causes.

"From what Rose has told me, you've been involved in some very high-profile corporate cases—that represented a great deal of money."

"Yes."

"I have to admit that what she described often sounded somewhat cold-blooded to me."

"It was. Hell, *I* was," he admitted. "The ultimate chess player orchestrating a high-stakes game. With millions of dollars at stake in that kind of litigation, I had no other choice."

"I find it difficult to believe that you've ever been cold-blooded. You're a very . . . passionate and intense man when you set your sights on a goal."

"I know." He studied her briefly. "I've destroyed the hopes of a lot of people over the years."

"Because you won most of your cases? Because you did your job well?"

He nodded.

"Let go of the guilt, Thomas. You can't change what's already happened."

"Words of wisdom?" he asked wryly.

Geneva shook her head. "Hardly. Just advice from a friend, that's all."

"What would happen if I suggested that you follow your own advice?"

She paused for a couple of seconds before answering him. "Believe it or not, I'm trying to."

"Is that why you asked me to leave the other night?"

"I was frightened," she said. "Very frightened."

"Of me?"

"Of course not!" she exclaimed.

"Geneva . . ."

She searched his face before conceding, "A little maybe."

"Why?"

"Because I know who and what I am, and you don't."

"I'm unshockable at this point in my life, or haven't you figured that out yet?"

A sad smile lifted the edges of her lips. "I wish I could believe that."

"Try," he urged.

"I'm not willing to be a notch on your bedpost, Thomas. Your aunt has been quite forthcoming about your conquests."

Her sudden and deliberate shift in conver-

sation amused him, but only to a small extent.
"You're dwelling on my past history."

"Am I? Do you remember that old cliché
about leopards and their spots?"

"You're trying to manufacture a smoke
screen. I know, because I've done it often
enough in court. I just don't understand your
motives, although I'd like to."

She shook her head. "There's really no
point in having this conversation."

He watched her get up from her chair, and
he saw the resignation in her face. She must
truly believe what she'd just said to him, even
though she couldn't have been more wrong.

Thomas snagged her hand as she attempted to walk past him. "Don't run away
from me, Geneva. Not this time."

After reading his lips, she glanced down at
his hand, then lifted her gaze to his face.

He released her, reluctantly.

She put some space between them before
she turned to look at him. "Running isn't necessary in my own home."

Thomas surged to his feet, but he didn't
approach her. He sensed the futility of touching her right now. "I care about you, dammit!"

"And I care about you," she responded,
her soft voice like an erotic caress. "But that
doesn't change some basic facts about my
life."

"Then let's try another approach."

"Like what?"

"A straightforward affair."

Clearly shocked, she demanded, "Are you crazy?"

"Only with wanting you and I know you want me. There's no way to get around that little reality, so let's do something about it once and for all."

She stood there and didn't say a word.

Her stunned silence prompted an admission that surprised even Thomas. "Rose was right. I have known a lot of women. They all knew the score where I was concerned. The sex was good. Sometimes, it was great. But those relationships . . . I finally stopped having them a few years ago because I didn't like how empty I felt after they ended. I want more. I need a hell of a lot more, especially at this point in my life."

"Thomas, we can't just use each other. It's not right."

"This isn't about using, Geneva. It's about mutual respect and admiration. It's about being happy, instead of lonely. It's about honest caring between two adults."

"I'm not the right woman for you," she insisted.

"You're the woman I want." *You're the woman I will have*, he thought. "You're the woman who belongs in my life and in my bed."

"Listen to me!" she exclaimed.

"I am listening, Geneva, and all I'm hearing is apprehension."

"Of course I'm apprehensive. Who wouldn't be? I don't want to get hurt."

"You care about me."

"Of course, I care, but . . ."

"Another smoke screen, Geneva?" he countered relentlessly.

"Stop this!" She closed her hands into fists, glaring at him.

"Deny it if you feel you have to, but you care about me in ways that surprise and unnerve you. And I care a hell of a lot about you. We'd be making love, not simply having sex. Tell me I'm wrong," he invited. "And then tell me you don't want me."

"This is the most ridiculous conversation I've ever had with a man!" she protested. "It ends right now."

He waved his hand dismissively. "Ending it won't solve a thing because I'll still want you and you'll still want me. And you'll still have the problem that you won't discuss with me. I respect you too much to unearth the truth through my own sources, but we both know I'm capable of doing just that if I'm forced to."

She gave him a look of sizzling outrage. "You'd have me investigated? How dare you!"

"I'll dare anything to stop your misguided attempt to slam the door on me."

"That's so cold-blooded."

"There's nothing even remotely chilly about what I want from you, Geneva. It's hot, combustible, and damn near about to drive me over the edge. I'm forty, not fourteen. I take you seriously, and I take the situation between us even more seriously. I expect you to afford me the same courtesy."

He watched her blink in surprise. "I do want you, Thomas. I'm barely sleeping through the night, I want you so much," she blurted out in that seductive low voice that echoed in his head when he was alone at night.

Finally! "Are you afraid of me?"

Although she seemed affected by the question, she shook her head.

"Good. We're making progress. Now, are you tired enough of the loneliness to do something about it?"

She hesitated.

"Are you?" he pressed.

"Yes, but I . . ."

Thank you, God, he thought. "Then why hesitate now?" he hammered right back.

"What if one of us falls in love? That would be disastrous."

I am falling in love, he realized suddenly. Oddly enough, he felt no apprehension, just a profound sense of certainty that he'd found his mate.

"Why don't we cross that bridge if and when we actually come to it?" he suggested, the self-confident and deadly calm litigator in evidence.

"I need to think about this."

"Fine. Think about it. I'll see you tomorrow at the store. You can give me your answer then."

Still looking stunned, Geneva preceded Thomas to the front door. Although he wanted to reassure her that she could trust him and his motives, he refrained. He knew she was reeling emotionally at the moment, and he'd never been the kind of man to overplay his hand. He loved her enough to take any and all risks, however.

After shrugging into his jacket and stepping into his boots, he turned, drew her against his body, and molded her to him so that she would have no doubt about his desire for her. Clasping her face between his palms, he kissed her. He kissed her at his leisure, as though he had all the time in the world to spare, and then some. He kissed her possessively, passionately, and with the kind of claim-staking thoroughness that spoke of the depth of his feelings for her. He released her with great reluctance, studied her intently for a lingering moment, and then jerked open the front door of the chalet.

As he strode to his car, he knew without glancing back that she still had her fingertips pressed to her lips, her body quaked with arousal, and her emotions were in complete disarray.

Thomas knew he'd shocked Geneva. Hell, he'd shocked himself, but he could no longer abide the secrets she insisted on keeping, the secrets that she used to keep him at a distance.

As far as Thomas Coltrane was concerned, tomorrow wouldn't arrive soon enough.

EIGHT

A heavy gust of icy wind pummeled Geneva as she made her way from her car to the shop the following morning. The cold air and single-digit mercury reading promised snow before the end of the day.

Shutting the front door behind her, Geneva deposited her purse on the counter and unbuttoned her heavy coat. When she spotted Rose, who came bustling out of the storeroom at top speed, she smiled. "Good morning. You're here bright and early."

Rose nodded. "It's a good thing. Those people from the Whitney Group in New York never look at a clock before they call us. They wanted to confirm their meeting with you for tomorrow morning. I told them you'd ring them back if anything interfered with the schedule."

"I'll call them first thing." Geneva grinned. "I still can't quite believe the negotiations have proceeded this far, but I'm definitely ready to see Talmadge, Inc. turn into a nationwide chain."

Rose pressed her hands together in front of her, her usual smile absent.

Geneva noticed her worried expression. "What's wrong? I thought you approved of all my plans for the business."

"Oh, I do, but there's a problem. Hadley Martin's secretary stopped by right after I got off the phone with the Whitney people. She was on her way to the hospital to see her boss."

"What's happened?" Geneva was alarmed because her attorney had a history of coronary problems.

"He's had a heart attack. It happened last night at his daughter's birthday party."

"How bad?"

"Moderate, according to the secretary, but Hadley's doctor has confined him to bed for the next week. It seems that he needs by-pass surgery, and if I know his wife as well as I think I do, then he'll be having it in short order."

"I'd better call New York. I can't move forward in the negotiations without Hadley, so I'll have to put everything on hold for the time being."

"That might not be necessary, Geneva," said the older woman, her gaze straying to the back of the store.

Geneva glanced in the same direction, then tensed as Thomas strolled out of her office, a file in his hand. Taking a deep breath to still her sudden uneasiness, she watched him approach.

He reminded her of a stalking predator. She already felt like his prey. After the previous night, a sleepless night during which she'd wrestled with her feelings and desire for Thomas, and now this situation with her lawyer, she didn't need any more complications.

After placing the file on a nearby counter, Thomas signed a greeting. "At the risk of sounding like an ambulance chaser, I think I can help."

She glanced at the file. Because she recognized the distinctive yellow folder, her gaze slashed to Rose, who flushed.

The older woman hurriedly explained, "Thomas stopped by this morning to help me move some heavy boxes in the storeroom. He was here when the call came in from New York and when Hadley's secretary stopped by. He put two and two together, so I thought he might be able to fill in for Hadley. The file was on your desk, and I didn't think you'd object if he took a look at it . . ." Her voice trailed off.

She knew Rose meant well, but Geneva felt trapped and more than a little annoyed at this invasion into her business affairs. *Affairs.* She winced inwardly, then decided that other people's good intentions would be her undoing.

"Why don't we sort this out in your office?" Thomas suggested. "Rose can handle your customers while we talk."

Two shoppers walked into the store as if on cue. Retrieving her purse, Geneva managed a curt nod and marched stiff-backed to the rear of the store.

Thomas picked up the file, gave Rose a reassuring look, and followed Geneva to her office.

Once she took off her coat and poured herself a cup of coffee, she took a seat at her desk and faced Thomas. He settled into a chair opposite her. She noticed that he didn't seem at all fazed by her obvious irritation with him. Blast the man!

"Don't be too upset with Rose," he said. "She was just trying to help."

"I'm not upset with her. I know *she* meant well."

"While I have an agenda?"

So much for stating the obvious, she thought. "Don't you?"

"Guilty, ma'am."

"You look positively thrilled with yourself, and not in the least repentant," she accused.

He chuckled, not bothering to issue a denial. "What I am is impressed. By you and Hadley Martin, who is an excellent attorney, by the way. He's orchestrated everything up until now in your favor. And it isn't as if the Whitney Group has a slouch in its executive staff. I know, because my partner dealt with them a few years back during an acquisition involving one of our clients. That said, it's clear that you're entering a critical stage in the negotiation process. The retention of control and the assurance of maintaining consistent standards in each store are obviously key issues at stake now."

Surprised and pleased by his accurate summary of the situation, Geneva nodded. "The first question I have to answer is whether I go it alone or put them off."

"Your other option is sitting across from you."

"I wouldn't want to impose."

"You aren't. I'm offering, and you'll get a bill for services rendered."

Geneva slowly exhaled.

Thomas got up from his chair and helped himself to a cup of coffee from the coffeemaker atop the file cabinet. His steady gaze on Geneva, he walked—no, he prowled back to his chair, although he didn't sit down.

"You've done this kind of thing before, I assume," she said, buying time in order to make the right decision.

The thought of entangling him in her professional life made her a tad uneasy. Not because she doubted his competence, but because she felt emotionally defenseless where he was concerned. And forget being obligated in any way, shape, or form to the man!

Thomas belatedly nodded in reply to her question as he settled back in his chair, then took a sip of coffee, and slid the mug onto her desk. "Many times, Geneva. It's a chess game, pure and simple."

"It's also a war of nerves, Counselor."

He grinned, looking almost boyish at the prospect of a major legal tussle. "I like a challenge, but you already know that, don't you?"

She ignored his question. It was personal, and they both knew it. "The meeting is tomorrow morning. Will that be enough time for you to prepare? I have additional information on the Whitney Group from Nicholas that you'll want to review."

"What about your partner? Does he have to approve my filling in?"

"How did you know I have a partner?"

"I've met him. Nice enough guy, from what I can tell. He doesn't say much, does he?"

She shook her head. "Sean is not involved

in the contract negotiations. I speak for both of us, and I hold his power of attorney for all business matters."

"Interesting partnership."

"It's not open for discussion," she informed him, slamming the door on anything to do with Sean Cassidy. Like Nicholas, Sean would always be the recipient of her absolute loyalty. To do otherwise would be a violation of everything she held dear.

"I'm impressed yet again."

"By what?"

"You, Ms. Talmadge."

Suspicious of his praise, Geneva asked, "Why?"

"Let's just say that I find your strength very seductive."

"Seductive?" she mused aloud. "Some men might not agree with you."

Thomas shrugged, but there was nothing even vaguely casual or careless about the gesture. "I'm not some men, Geneva. You don't ever want to forget that. We're on the same wavelength, and that's all that counts between us. The rest of the world isn't that important to me. You are."

"If you say so," she said, unwilling to follow his lead since she felt certain that he was heading toward the subject of their becoming lovers.

"I say so." His eyes gleamed with a kind of

adamance that left little doubt that he really meant what he'd just said. "Now, as to the other matter between us."

Geneva stiffened.

"I'm officially tabling that discussion until a more appropriate time. You need to focus on the Whitney Group for now."

She didn't move a muscle or make a sound as he drained his coffee, got to his feet, and picked up the file. She simply watched him, trying hard to maintain an even expression that concealed the tumultuous state of her emotions.

Thomas looked at her expectantly.

She was nonplussed for a moment, then realized he was waiting for the file Nicholas had assembled for her use. She slid it across the top of her desk, her eyes on his face the entire time, and then tucked her hands in her lap.

He collected the second file, his gaze speculative. He then spoke slowly enough for her to read his lips. "I'll stop in later."

Once he disappeared from sight, Geneva muttered a word she rarely used, then surged to her feet and made her way into the store-room. Jerking on a smock, she threw herself into the task of redoing the display window.

It was an all-day chore, but it did little to distract her from her thoughts of Thomas. She still possessed a great deal of unspent nervous energy when he reappeared at the end of the workday.

She had just positioned the Closed sign in the newly decorated and well-lighted display window, which now reflected the Thanksgiving season. Pulling open the front door, she waved him inside. He placed his briefcase on the countertop next to the cash register and pulled off his gloves.

"I can't stay long. I have a dinner meeting with a client."

Disappointment crashed over her like an avalanche, stunning her. Geneva recovered quickly, though. "I'm busy, too. What did you need?" she asked.

Thomas peered down at her, a half smile hovering around his lips and heat in his gaze as his eyes swept over her. "I don't think you want me to answer that question right now."

"I assumed you were here because of the Whitney Group." She was determined to ignore his personal asides.

Thomas shook his head as he stepped closer. "You're going to fight me every step of the way, aren't you?"

Geneva shot a belligerent look at him as she squared her shoulders. He kept moving forward, his eyes darkly sensual as they roamed over her face and then down her body. Her breasts swelled as his gaze lingered on them, and she felt her nipples pucker into points of throbbing need. Geneva trembled, but she didn't give ground.

The closer he got, the more she had to tilt her head back to keep her gaze fastened on his face. She closed her hands into fists. The urge to touch him was like a reckless current within her. It made her ache.

"Relax, Geneva. I couldn't harm you even if it meant saving my own life," he said before he drew her into his arms and held her.

Relax? How do I relax when I'm tied up in knots? she wondered, then felt all of her resistance to his embrace drain out of her as his hands gently roved up and down her narrow back.

He soothed with his touch.

He comforted.

He reassured.

Geneva sagged against him, overwhelmed by the desire coiling deep inside her, by the strength he seemed so willing to share with her, and finally by the reality that she had fallen in love with him.

She shivered, then slipped her arms around his waist, tucked her face into the warm curve of his neck, and breathed in the musky scent of cologne. The wool lapel of his topcoat tickled her chin, but she didn't draw back. She couldn't. She wanted him too much, wanted everything he had to offer as a man.

She felt the power of his desire for her as

she moved closer, aligning her entire body to his. When his arms tightened around her, she silently reveled in the safety she found in his embrace.

He pressed his lips to her forehead.

Geneva nearly wept, because she felt cherished for the very first time in her life.

A tremor suddenly ripped through his entire body. An answering tremor rippled through hers.

Regret filled her heart several moments later when he released her, but she marshaled her wits as she met his gaze.

"The meeting is at nine," she said. "I've arranged for a private conference room at the inn. The hotel restaurant staff will serve refreshments during the meeting, then our lunch when we call for it."

"Do you want me to pick you up in the morning?" he asked, all business once again.

She shook her head. "I'll meet you there. Just ask the concierge for directions when you arrive at the inn."

Thomas extended his hand and briefly stroked her cheek with shaking fingers.

Unable to stop herself, Geneva turned her face into his palm. Her eyes fluttered closed. Her lips brushed over his skin. A breathless exhalation issued from him.

Glancing at Thomas, she glimpsed the tension in his clenched jaw just before he drove the long, narrow fingers of both his hands into her hair. He anchored her head between his palms and leaned down, the intensity of his gaze enough to scorch her soul.

Geneva held perfectly still, her eyes wide, the air in her lungs trapped, burning for release.

He claimed her mouth.

She welcomed his possession, her lips parting, and he proceeded to thoroughly reacquaint himself with the wet heat of her mouth.

Geneva could barely stand when their kiss ended. Flushed and shaking with desire, she seized the edge of the counter to steady herself.

"Tomorrow," Thomas said before collecting his briefcase.

She nodded, but this time she refused to watch him walk away. She feared that she might run after him.

Geneva eventually found the strength to walk to the door and secure the lock. As she stood there with her forehead resting against the glass pane, all the fight rushed out of her. Her willingness to continue living in isolation followed a few seconds later.

She knew in that moment that two things had finally happened: she'd resurrected the courage necessary to risk her emotions, and Thomas would soon become her lover.

The twin realizations unnerved her a little,

because she had no idea where this journey would lead her, but the unknown no longer frightened her. She'd moved well beyond fear. Now, she possessed the strength to venture forward, to reach out and seize with both hands the promise of happiness, even if it only turned out to be a brief interlude in her life.

Thomas strolled into the conference room at the Cedar Grove Inn the following morning like a warrior armed for battle. Geneva watched him from her position at the wall of windows that overlooked the scores of skiers lined up at the lift at the base of Cedar Mountain.

Thomas joined her at the window once he placed his briefcase and topcoat on the conference table. "Looks tempting, doesn't it?"

"Very tempting, and definitely a low-stress way to spend a day."

"We'll have to join the hordes on the mountain one of these weeks."

She smiled, surprised by how relaxed she felt despite the negotiations scheduled to commence in less than ten minutes. "I'd like that. Rose told me you competed when you were younger."

"Much younger. Seems like it all happened in another lifetime." Unbuttoning his suit jacket, Thomas shoved his hands into his trouser pockets and rocked back on his heels. "My competition days ended when I graduated from college and headed east for law school. I'm pretty rusty now."

"I haven't been out this year yet. No time."

"Then let's make some time."

The door opened, and four men and two women came in. Thomas strode across the room and introduced himself as Geneva's temporary counsel.

The day lasted forever. At least, that's how Geneva felt that evening as she stood in front of the family room fireplace at Thomas's lodge. She stared at the darting flames and absently massaged her right shoulder.

Thomas stroked her shoulder to signal his presence behind her.

Geneva turned to face him.

"You all right?"

"Just tired." She smiled. "Being fed helped, though. Thank you for dinner."

"You didn't think Rose was the only chef in the family, did you?"

She laughed. "I hadn't given it much thought, to be quite honest." Geneva accepted the snifter of brandy he handed her.

"I'm full of surprises."

"I think I've figured out that much about you." She took a sip of cognac, placed the snifter on the coffee table, and then sank into one of two chairs before the fireplace.

"You surprised me, you know," he said. "I didn't think you'd accept my dinner invitation."

"I was hungry."

Thomas grimaced. "Trying to deflate my ego?"

"It could use a puncture or two," she informed him.

"Ouch!"

"Need a bandage?" she quipped.

Thomas made himself comfortable in the adjacent chair. "I'll live."

"We need to discuss their latest counteroffer, don't we?" she asked, pushing them on to the real reason they were spending the evening together. "What did you think?"

"About what?"

"Today, of course."

"At the moment, I'm thinking about you, not work."

"Thomas," she warned.

"We've got twelve hours before the next meeting," he reminded her.

"Then we should spend the time productively."

"We will," he said as he got to his feet.

He towered over her, his hand extended.

She stared up at him, her heart racing.

"I want to make love to you," he said. "I need to make love with you."

Geneva hesitated, momentarily startled by his admission, but she reminded herself that she wanted the same thing. Trembling, she reached out to accept his hand.

He tugged her to her feet. "Trust me," he urged.

She smiled, said softly, "I do trust you," and moved forward.

As she felt his arms circle her body, Geneva knew she'd finally found a home for her heart. Whether it was a permanent or a temporary home seemed unimportant, because she loved Thomas, loved him so completely that she doubted the day would ever come when she didn't love him.

NINE

"What are you thinking?" Thomas said as they stood facing each other in the master suite of the lodge a few minutes later.

"I'm not thinking," Geneva replied after a moment of hesitation. "I'm feeling."

"Then tell me what you're feeling."

She smiled. "You actually want a list?"

Thomas chuckled. "I want *you*. The list can wait until later."

Her smile faded. She reached out to him, whispering, "I'm glad."

He took her hands, lifted them one at a time to his lips, and pressed hot kisses into her palms. He felt the tremors that moved through her, saw the surprise and desire that widened her blue eyes and flushed her cheeks.

Geneva shifted closer once he freed her hands. Slowly she slid her palms up his arms to his shoulders, then around his neck before tangling her fingers at his nape.

Going up on tiptoes, she pressed against him. Her breasts plumped against his chest and her hips brushed teasingly against his groin. A tremulous sigh escaped her to wash across his neck.

Thomas closed his eyes, savoring the lush feel of her, feeling the jolt of desire travel throughout his body. Geneva tantalized and teased as she shifted even nearer to perfect the alignment of their two bodies. An instant later she kissed him, tentatively at first, then with greater confidence.

Thomas welcomed her tender aggression. His hands snagged around her narrow waist, his fingertips almost meeting. Angling his head, he deepened their kiss, his tongue plunging into her mouth to explore the heated terrain beyond her teeth.

Geneva gasped, then moaned into his mouth as he smoothed his hands over her hips. He held her still, rubbing against her, his already aroused body growing even more aroused.

Time seemed to stop as they rocked against each other.

On fire for her, Thomas longed to bury himself within her body and remain there forever. He knew it would be the ultimate fulfillment of every fantasy he'd ever had about

Geneva, not simply the sweetest kind of pleasure he would ever experience.

He devoured her mouth, his rigid control in jeopardy and his hunger for her escalating as his imagination went wild. He couldn't get enough of the taste of her now that she'd stopped resisting.

He didn't understand all the reasons for her sudden capitulation. He didn't care at that moment. They were together. For now that was enough. Later he would eventually need answers to all of his questions about this woman.

Geneva surged against him, matching his intense desire with her own. Her hands grew frantic as they moved over his shoulders and chest, her mouth voracious as she responded to his searching kisses.

Thomas had never wanted a woman more than he wanted Geneva Talmadge. He wanted her naked, though. He needed her naked, needed to touch her everywhere and memorize each curve and hollow of her hourglass-shaped body before he took her. An unexpected thought suddenly pierced his consciousness—he would never *not* need this woman.

Tearing his lips from hers, Thomas lifted his head, dragged in enough air to feed his starving lungs, and peered down at her. His breathing sounded ragged, and he noticed that his hands shook from the intense physical and emotional cravings Geneva inspired. They pounded through his veins with the force of a steadily advancing tide.

He felt her tremble as he began to free the buttons that ran down the front of her fitted gray sweater dress. Once he completed the task, he peeled the fabric away from her body, his breath catching in his throat when he glimpsed the black lace bra and matching panties she wore. Black silk stockings encased the length of her shapely legs, allowing a tantalizing view of pale skin at the top of each thigh.

Thomas freed the catch at the front of her bra. He watched the flimsy garment gape partially open.

She reached up and parted the delicate fabric. Her full breasts tumbled free. She shrugged out of the lacy confection, her gaze locked on his face as it fell to the floor to join her dress.

He saw the pulse throbbing in the hollow of her throat, leaned down, and trailed the tip of his tongue over the spot. Straightening, Thomas cupped her breasts, their weight and the satiny smoothness of her skin so enticing that his groin throbbed in concert with his hammering pulse.

Geneva's eyes fell closed. She arched into his hands, her nipples beading into tight little knots that stabbed at his palms. Soft sounds spilled past her lips as he plucked at her nipples with his fingertips.

Thomas heard her shattered gasp, then the long low moan that followed when he leaned down and covered the tip of one breast with his mouth. As he suckled forcefully, he trailed his fingertips down her back, slipped his hands beneath the lace that covered her hips, and cupped her buttocks.

He dropped to his knees, sliding her lace panties down her legs. He steadied her swaying body as she kicked aside the delicate garment. He then smoothed his palms up her silk-covered legs, but he didn't make any attempt to remove her stockings. They hugged her legs without the aid of a garter belt, and served as an erotic counterpoint to her nakedness.

He bracketed her hips with his hands, his lips whispering over the gentle swell of her abdomen. Painting her skin with the wet heat of his tongue, he crisscrossed the lower half of her body until he reached the silky golden nest at the top of her thighs.

He felt her fingers dig into his shoulders as he nudged her thighs apart, then heard her moan as he branded her with his intimate kisses.

When he slid a fingertip along the humid folds of her femininity, he found her slick with desire. He kissed her there again, the tip of his tongue tracing the damp seam of her femininity. The taste of her was an aphrodisiac, one he didn't ever want to live without.

Surging to his feet, Thomas gathered her into the heat of his powerful body and reclaimed her mouth. She began tugging at the buttons of his shirt, but her fingers shook clumsily, and, after several moments of frustration, she uttered an inarticulate cry of frustration into his mouth.

Thomas jerked the fabric apart, uncaring that several buttons popped off and dropped to the floor in his haste to have her hands on his skin. He shed his shirt, freed the buckle of his belt, and unzipped his trousers without releasing her lips.

She drove her fingers into the dense dark hair that covered his muscular chest, her tongue simultaneously darting into the recesses of his mouth, taunting and teasing until Thomas thought he might go mad from the desire roaring through his body like an out-of-control freight train.

Shuddering, he tore his mouth free, stepped out of his trousers and briefs, and bent down to jerk off his socks.

Geneva eagerly moved back into his arms, molding herself against him like a second skin.

Lifting her up, he smoothed her legs around his hips.

With her arms twined around his neck, Geneva moved from side to side, her full, taut-tipped breasts brushing repeatedly across his chest, her pelvis lightly stroking his erection.

Their lips met and fused again and again, their mouths mating with a kind of ravenous hunger that defied reason and restraint.

As he inhaled her breathless cries and tasted her hunger for him, Thomas carried her the few steps to his bed. Seated on the edge, he kept her perched atop his powerful thighs, her legs still circling his narrow hips.

Geneva pulled back without warning. She watched Thomas from beneath half-lowered lashes as she trailed her fingertips down his chest, past the ridged expanse of muscle that covered his belly, and then slipped her hands between their bodies.

Thomas tensed, inhaling sharply when he felt her touch. She circled his pulsing sex with her fingers, her touch curious at first, then more confident as she measured his length and thickness. She tantalized him with long, slow strokes that set his senses aflame and made it nearly impossible for him to breathe.

"Be careful," he said.

Geneva smiled, a slow, scintillating smile that sent molten sensations rushing into his loins.

She shimmied forward, her gaze still on

him as she guided their lower bodies to an intimate kiss. Clasping him with both hands, Geneva moaned, the sound coming from low in her throat as she rocked against his hard flesh.

She amazed.

She tempted.

She tormented.

And she seduced.

Take me, her expression and her body simultaneously invited. *Take me now*.

Thomas shuddered with barely contained violence.

"I want you inside of me," Geneva finally managed to say.

Unable to restrain himself, Thomas grasped her hips, stood, and then tumbled her backward to the mattress. As he came down over her, he protected her from being crushed by resting the weight of his upper body on his elbows.

"I need you," he said slowly enough for her to read his lips.

Without speaking, Geneva reached up and trailed her fingertips across his cheek. The simple gesture conveyed both willingness and a wealth of emotions.

He turned his head, capturing a fingertip and sucking it deeply into his mouth. He felt the quiver that rippled through her as he swirled his tongue around the slender digit.

Her hips stirred with what Thomas recognized as restless and, as yet, unappeased desire. Determined to draw out the experience ahead of them, he lowered his head and took her lips. He thrust his tongue into her mouth, drinking in the taste of her.

They both gasped for air when he lifted his head a few minutes later.

Thomas shifted to one side and reached for the drawer of the nightstand on the far side of the bed.

As if sensing his intent, Geneva caught his arm. "I trust you, Thomas, and you can trust me."

Nodding, he gathered her into his arms again and held her, trying to control the craving for fruition that continued to threaten his control.

Geneva trembled beneath him, her fingers digging into his hips.

Thomas felt her growing tension and met her gaze. The tears that seeped from the corners of her eyes and trailed across her temples startled him.

"What, love?"

"I want you," she choked out. "Now."

He reacted instinctively to her almost pain-filled plea, realizing that no woman had ever made him feel more desired or more male.

He drove into her a heartbeat later, primal

and territorial impulses guiding him as he penetrated the snug channel of her body.

She cried out, clutching at him. Thomas recognized the sound for what it was. Relief and recognition, not pain. He heard the same cry of relief and recognition echo within his own soul as he succumbed to the compelling need to possess this woman.

Geneva gripped his shoulders and circled his hips with her silk-covered legs as he repeatedly plunged into her. The sensations caused by the fabric as it slid over his skin heightened his already stimulated senses. His heart raced and the blood pounding through his veins scalded.

Geneva writhed beneath Thomas. She felt alive, more alive than she'd felt in years. She nearly wept with amazement.

She met his every thrust with an upward thrust of her own. Her body clenched ever so tightly, then quivered around him. She gloried in the pleasure she found in his intimate embrace, and she savored the force of his erection each time he drove deeply into her. Anointing the side of his neck and his chest with feverish kisses, she clung to him as their pace steadily increased.

Geneva felt her insides start to quicken. The suddenness of the spasms spun her into a whirling vortex of sensations that overwhelmed any control she might have wished to exercise.

Her need escalated with every passing second. She twisted and turned, seeking, searching for fruition.

Thomas altered the angle and depth of his penetration as he cradled her against his chest. He simultaneously duplicated the pumping motion of his lower body with his darting tongue.

Geneva felt poised on the edge of a steep cliff, ready to leap into a freefall of glittering sensory delights that only Thomas could provide. She surged upward, the release he promised within reach.

It came without warning, and a stunned cry spilled out of her as something shattered deep inside her body. The sensations spread outward, consuming, devastating.

Geneva surrendered to the inevitable. She had already surrendered herself to Thomas. She rode a wave of pure, mind-numbing pleasure in the moments that followed, while spasms continued to ripple through her body. She called out his name. Over and over again.

Thomas eased his pace, drew in a ragged breath, then stopped moving altogether.

Geneva held tightly to him, momentarily disoriented. When she realized what he was doing, she appreciated the generosity of his restraint. It confused her a little, however. She peered up at him, her eyes still glazed and her lower body still trembling in the aftermath of climax.

He lifted one hand so that she could see it, and finger-spelled, "You're amazing."

She didn't understand why he thought so, but she smiled anyway. "If you say so." She shifted beneath him, her gaze still on his face. Muscles deep inside her body quivered involuntarily around his flesh.

Groaning, Thomas clamped his jaws together. He finally muttered, "I say so."

Geneva read his lips, her smile widening at the pleasure he found in her response to him as a lover. She caught her breath and her heart slowed to a less-than-breakneck speed. She shifted beneath him. Experimentally this time. She watched his eyes fall closed, then noticed the tension that caused a muscle to flutter high in his cheek.

She felt the throbbing power of his desire, and she rocked her hips, the subtle movement eliciting a pulsing response. Aroused by the feel of him inside of her body, she intensified her movement as she wrapped her arms around his shoulders.

After several breathless minutes, Thomas stilled her undulations by pressing her hips against the mattress. He captured her attention with his piercing gaze, the expression on his face assuring her that he understood her invitation.

She cradled his face between her palms and urged him closer. Nibbling on his lips, she shimmied her hips in a timeless mating summons.

Thomas didn't disappoint her.

He surged more deeply into her, paused, and then teasingly invaded and withdrew with unhurried movements.

Geneva sighed into his mouth, matching his slow-motion thrusts. She stroked the length of his back, then cupped his hips with both hands, her fingertips flexing against the warmth of his skin. She simultaneously bathed his inner lower lip with taunting swipes of her tongue, then sucked at it before worrying the damp expanse with gentle teeth.

He suddenly jerked against her. His restraint vanished. His answering kiss was possessive and ruthless as he pumped into her with increased force.

Geneva followed his lead.

Willingly.

Eagerly.

She wanted everything Thomas offered, and she wanted to give everything of herself.

She loved him, loved him more deeply than she'd ever loved anyone in her life. That thought struck her as her inner core quivered uncontrollably and her body began to tighten once more.

They took the journey together this time.

His muscular body knotted with tension, Thomas tore his mouth free and struggled for air. He trapped Geneva's hands above her head. Still writhing beneath him, she drew her knees up and locked her ankles at the base of his spine.

Thomas felt the increased snugness of her body, the clutching sensations caused by her bent knees and upraised legs driving him to the edge of madness. He pounded into her.

She suddenly screamed.

Thomas savored the sound and sight and feel of her passion as she threw back her head, stiffened, and then completely came apart beneath him. Her quivering body, the subsequent moans torn from her depths, and her sustained release destroyed his control, once and for all.

She embraced him when he collapsed atop her a short while later, her lips whispering kisses over his face and neck.

He couldn't speak yet, so he didn't try to articulate the emotions cascading over him. He promised himself that they would talk in the morning.

They drifted lazily in the aftermath of what they'd just shared.

Thomas eventually rolled onto his side,

Geneva cradled against his chest and their bodies still intimately linked. He dragged a quilt over them, then tenderly kissed her. She spoke softly, but he failed to make out the words as he fell into a doze.

Shortly after midnight Thomas relinquished his hold on Geneva long enough to put a match to the logs and kindling already arranged in the fireplace. He felt her gaze on him as he made his way back to bed. She opened her arms to him in a gesture of welcome when he sat down beside her.

They made love once again, their passion as incendiary as the flames consuming the logs in the fireplace, then fell asleep with their arms around each other.

Geneva awakened suddenly, her heart racing with panic until she realized where she was. Her panic increased tenfold as the achiness in her body reminded her of the night of intimacy she'd just experienced with Thomas.

The ramifications of her behavior hit her like a blow. She'd welcomed Thomas into her heart and her body, and the consequences of her actions were inescapable.

If their relationship continued, she would have to tell him about her past. She hated the very thought of revealing the truth, despite the fact that she felt weighted down by the burden that had caused her reclusive life in the first place.

In the minutes that followed she decided that it would be best if she left before Thomas woke up. He read her moods too well, and she doubted her ability to conceal her escalating uneasiness. She needed to be composed when they finally talked.

He slept beside her, his breathing deep and steady. Geneva pressed a kiss to his shoulder before she slipped away from him. She paused in the darkness, trying to remember where she'd left her clothes.

She crept soundlessly out of the bedroom, gathering articles of clothing scattered on the floor along the way. Once she made her way downstairs, she hurriedly dressed, collected her purse, and put on her coat. She knew she'd behaved impulsively, and she said as much in a quickly penned note to Thomas that she left on the kitchen counter beside the coffeemaker.

Geneva drove the narrow winding mountain road to her chalet. The dawn lightened the sky as she parked her Jeep and made her way indoors. The hot shower she took did nothing to restore her composure. She felt exhausted, emotionally and physically. Despite the temptation to cancel the meeting scheduled that morning with the Whitney Group, she forced herself back into the car an hour later and drove into Cedar Grove to face the Whitney Group and Thomas Coltrane.

Thomas awoke shortly before dawn to a missing woman and a cold bed. He found a note in the kitchen, a note that chilled his soul.

She'd written: "We acted impulsively last night. It was a mistake."

Thomas had feared that Geneva might suffer from morning-after regrets, but he hadn't expected her to run from him without an attempt to discuss the situation. His instincts assured him that her past had reared its ugly head. Whatever she was hiding, he felt certain that it was serious, perhaps more serious than he'd originally thought.

He put a tight rein on his anger, vowing to know the truth—the whole truth. The experienced attorney, the relentless, calculating, often ruthless man who'd rarely suffered a defeat in the courtroom, made the decision he hadn't wanted to make. Unfortunately, Geneva had forced his hand.

Thomas telephoned a trusted friend, took him into his confidence, and shared what little he knew about Geneva Talmadge. His friend wryly remarked that Thomas had fallen in with a unique crowd since leaving San Diego. Following that cryptic observation, he then promised a prompt reply to Thomas's inquiry.

As Thomas began his preparations for the meeting with the Whitney Group, he told himself that Geneva would never have allowed them to become lovers if she hadn't cared about him.

He refused to let her close her heart to him. Not now. What he felt for her went far beyond simple caring. He loved her, and he didn't intend to lose her.

TEN

Geneva looked as emotionally stressed as he felt, Thomas decided when he strolled into the conference room at the inn later that morning. He'd deliberately delayed his arrival, waiting until all parties were assembled before making his entrance.

Despite the urge to deal with their personal problems as quickly as possible, he didn't. His confrontation with Geneva would take place later, when he was ready and only after he'd heard from his friend in Washington.

Thomas greeted everyone, including Geneva, with a brusque nod. After discarding his topcoat, he took a seat at the head of the conference table, wordlessly stating that he was in charge. And he proved it by orchestrating the contract negotiations with a steel-nerved precision that validated his reputation for ruthlessness.

Although Thomas recognized Geneva's distracted emotional state for what it was, he took pride in the fact that she held her own during the nonstop seven-hour meeting. She allowed him, in his capacity as her legal representative, to hammer out her terms, one point at a time. Because they had settled on the tactic prior to the start of the talks, she inserted herself into the process at designated junctures.

By the conclusion of the meeting, her goals for Talmadge, Inc. were itemized and approved by the parties present. Final approval of the contract would take place when the conglomerate held its quarterly board meeting the following week, but that approval was a foregone conclusion in the minds of everyone in the room.

Thomas felt her worried glances though he gave no indication of them. Tension emanated from her. He knew she had a headache by the manner in which her fingertips strayed to her temples, but she refused his offer of an aspirin.

He treated her nonchalantly throughout the day, purposefully giving her the impression that having a woman flee his bed in the middle of the night didn't bother him in the least. The appearance of indifference cost him, however, and the men and women facing him across the negotiating table bore the brunt of his frustration with Geneva.

Because the Whitney Group representatives had a corporate jet waiting for them at a nearby airport, they all agreed that their success would be celebrated at the signing of the formal contract in New York later in the month.

Thomas remained alert to Geneva's every move as the meeting concluded and everyone retrieved their belongings.

Geneva put on her coat, reclaimed her purse and briefcase, and made her way to the door of the conference room. She almost managed to edge out of the room on the heels of the visiting executives, but Thomas, having anticipated her escape plan, foiled it when he caught her arm and halted her exit.

"I need to get back to the shop," Geneva said, her gaze on the others as they disappeared down the hallway.

Thomas placed his fingertips beneath her chin and turned her face so that she could see him. He already knew that Rose, along with a seasonal helper whom Geneva had just hired, was taking care of the store.

"I'll go with you," he said, holding back the annoyance he felt. "I have to stop in at my office."

She nodded, her reluctance so obvious that

Thomas wanted to take her by the shoulders and shake some sense into her. He quelled the impulse, however, and remained in control.

Geneva didn't speak at all as they left the hotel and walked the half mile to the converted Victorian mansion in the fading, late afternoon light. Her silence didn't surprise Thomas.

The day-long snowfall had dusted everything in white and crunched beneath their feet. The crisp mountain air held the promise of additional precipitation that night.

Geneva paused in front of the entrance to her store. After slinging the straps of her purse and briefcase across her shoulder, she lifted her hands, "Thank you for handling the contract."

"You're welcome," he responded grimly.

"Send me your bill."

"There won't be one." With that, Thomas turned and walked away.

Geneva hurried after him as he made his way down the sidewalk and into the main lobby of the building.

"Thomas!"

He ignored her, proceeded up the stairs to his office, and unlocked the door to the waiting room. Geneva followed him, which was the response he'd intended to provoke with his abruptness.

He pushed open the door and flipped the

light switch, then deposited his briefcase and topcoat on a chair. "Close the door, will you?"

Geneva did as he requested, then moved hesitantly into the room. "Why won't there be a bill?" she asked.

Thomas noticed the sheet of paper in the basket attached to the fax machine. Instead of answering Geneva, he walked over to the credenza, scanned the fax, and then folded the sheet of paper and tucked it into the breast pocket of his suit jacket.

The information he'd just received was sketchy, but Thomas grasped the bottom line. Geneva Talmadge had once functioned as some kind of an overseas operative for the government and under the guidance of Nicholas Benteen. Further data would have to be given in a face-to-face meeting with his friend, which implied that the work she'd done was highly classified.

Thomas concluded that her connection to the terrorist Jamal wasn't an accident of fate, and he couldn't help wondering what kind of deadly covert games she'd been involved in prior to settling in Cedar Grove. Because he had no plans to fly to Washington in order to obtain the truth, he realized that the most important information he needed had to come from Geneva herself. He intended to have it. Sooner, rather than later.

"Why, Thomas? Why won't there be a bill?" she asked once again.

He turned and drilled her with a fury-filled look. He then finger-spelled four simple words. "Last night covered it."

She looked like a woman who'd just taken a blow from a well-aimed fist.

Thomas drew little satisfaction from her response, but he didn't cease and desist. Too much was at stake. "Wasn't that your intent?" he demanded, his hands slashing through the air as he ignored her shock. "Your body in exchange for services rendered?"

Her usual poise completely absent, Geneva shook her head in denial.

"What was your intent?" he asked.

She followed him as he strode into his inner office.

"Or was last night just a one-night stand? One of those no harm, no foul kind of nights between consenting adults?"

She stared at him, looking stunned as she lingered just inside the doorway.

"Do I finally have your attention, Geneva?"

She gathered herself under his watchful gaze. He watched her do it by sheer force of will, and he grudgingly admired her strength as she squared her slender shoulders and lifted her chin.

She signed, "You have my attention. Cruelty does that to me."

"What you did wasn't cruel?" he demanded.

She paled and made her way to the nearest chair. She sank into it, her purse and briefcase thudding to the floor at her feet.

Thomas approached her, drew her up from the chair, and relieved her of her coat. Taking Geneva by the hand, he led her into the private sitting room adjacent to his office. He didn't pause until they stood in front of the couch positioned before the fireplace. "Have a seat."

Geneva slowly lowered herself onto the couch. She moved with the caution of a very wary woman as she perched on the edge of the cushion.

Thomas towered over her, forcing her to look up at him. "Talk to me, Geneva. It's time."

"About what?" she stalled.

"Your past. That's the boulder you've dragged back into the path of our relationship, isn't it?"

She pressed her fingertips to her temples. "You make it sound so easy. It's not."

"It would be if you trusted me."

"But I do."

"Prove it." He rose and went to the mantelpiece, his eyes still on her.

She understood his meaning. She looked away, her hands still in her lap while she spoke, "I'm not ready. Not yet, anyway."

Tears brimmed in her large blue eyes. She fought the urge to weep as she watched Thomas light the already prepared logs in the fireplace. What would be the point in revealing her past? she wondered. The truth would end things between them once and for all, and she wasn't ready for that. She wanted more of this man. Needed more, especially after the night they'd just shared.

"Come here," Thomas said.

"Why?" she whispered.

"I need to touch you, if only to prove to you that I'm real and that I'm not going anywhere."

Filled with a combination of anguish and hope, she reached out to him, wanting to believe that he spoke the truth, desperate to believe that the woman she'd become during the last several years somehow compensated for what she'd once been.

Thomas took her hands and drew her closer. He sat down on the couch, settled her into his lap, and held her. His hands drifting up and down her back, he unknowingly soothed her with the kind of tenderness that also seduced.

In the minutes that followed Geneva realized that she possessed the courage to risk everything. The time to tell the truth had arrived. Honesty forced her to admit to herself that she felt no shame about her past.

If anything, she felt resigned to the reality of why and how she had become an explosives expert in the first place. She was, after all, Patrick Talmadge's daughter. Because she'd been his companion during those nomadic years, wandering the globe in search of conflict, it wasn't surprising that she'd perfected her skills under his tutelage.

To deny her past meant that she had to deny her father, and her conscience wouldn't allow her to do that, not even for Thomas Coltrane. Thomas might reject her, but she knew she would survive. She'd survived much worse. Invariably sadder, and always much wiser. But still standing, still loved by her family, and still in possession of her self-respect.

She'd managed to avoid rejection for years, although the safety of her reclusive life had cost her the dream of loving and being loved for herself that she'd once nurtured. Thomas had brought those dreams back to life, but he also had the power to destroy them even if he didn't realize it.

Geneva lifted her face from the warm curve of his neck and met his gaze. Any words she might have uttered died unspoken when Thomas cupped the back of her head and guided her lips to his. He kissed her then, his mouth possessive as he drank in her shocked exhalation.

He wrenched free of her just moments later, muttering, "If seducing you is the only way to get you to talk to me, then so be it."

Gasping for breath, Geneva tried to tell him that she didn't understand what he'd just said, but he reclaimed her mouth, silencing her. Her hunger for him exploded across the landscape of her senses like a firestorm. A voice in her head reminded her that this might be their last time together, and she refused to deny herself.

She lost her ability to think or reason clearly under his passionate onslaught. She eagerly succumbed to the darting penetration of his tongue as it invaded her mouth and the roaming of his hands over her body.

She even forgot that they were in the sitting room of his office. She cared about nothing but Thomas, because he had become the center of her universe.

Tasting him, touching him, and destroying any boundaries, real or imagined, between them became her focus. She matched his thrusting tongue stroke for stroke, her hands frantic as she tore at the buttons of his shirt. This time she needed no assistance as she parted the fabric and plunged her fingers into the dense hair that covered his chest.

He groaned in response to her touch, then

caught the hem of her sweater, dragged it up and over her head, and cast it aside. His hands went immediately to the catch at the front of her bra. Flicking it open, he palmed her breasts as they sprang free.

Geneva gasped, then moaned as she felt his fingertips plucking at her nipples. They peaked instantly, tight mauve knots of pure sensation.

Without relinquishing his mouth, she shifted atop him and positioned herself astride his thighs. She inched forward, her pelvis nudging against his swelling groin, the interior of her body already moistening in anticipation of the joining she longed for. She reached down, stroking the hardness covered by his trousers. He pulsed under her touch, enflaming her, tempting her.

Thomas jerked beneath her fingertips. He surged up from the couch with Geneva still locked in his arms. He kept their lips fused even as he freed himself of his clothing, then stripped what remained of hers from her lower body.

He brought her down atop him as he sprawled across the couch, his hands closing over her breasts, his mouth voracious as he scoured the interior of hers with swipes of his tongue. He drank deeply of her, saturating his senses with the flavor of her. His hands shook as he caressed her.

She clutched at his shoulders as she brought herself to her knees and crouched over him. Slowly lowering her hips, she tantalized him with sensual arching strokes of her pelvis against his maleness. She felt the surging power in his loins as his flesh quivered against the damp folds of her femininity.

Geneva brought her hips even closer, taking him partway into her body with a smooth gliding motion. She watched his face, saw the tension there, saw as well the desire that had darkened his eyes. She loved him, so deeply, so completely, that she knew in that instant that it would break her heart to lose him.

"Now," he insisted.

Geneva read the word as it passed his lips, then smiled before dipping downward and completely impaling herself with his strength. A shattered sound escaped her as she settled atop him, their bodies fully merged now.

She undulated, slowly, teasingly, her body quivering as she moved. He smoothed his fingers down the front of her body, dragged his knuckles across her lower abdomen, then clamped his hands like brackets on her hips. He held her still.

She felt his strength and savored it. She leaned forward, pressing hot little kisses to his neck, then shifting to his chin, where she gently nibbled. She felt like purring, and did exactly that as she tormented and teased him with tilting motions of her hips.

He claimed her lips in the same instant that he surged upward into her. He caught her stunned gasp, inhaling it as he guided the movement of her lower body.

Geneva felt every inch of his penetrating length, felt the pulsing power of his desire as it throbbed within her. She trembled, her body starting to tighten. She felt as though she might break apart at any moment, and she gloried in the feeling, just as she gloried in the act of intimacy they now shared.

She rode him then, the tension within her body spiraling tighter and tighter. Her pace steadily increased, not by design but as a result of the urgency she felt.

Thomas simultaneously ate at her mouth and pounded into her, his hunger driving him. She tore her lips free, arching atop him as her insides suddenly quickened. Soft cries escaped her, intensifying as she bucked against him.

He drew her forward, covered one breast with his hand and took the nipple of the other one into his mouth. He sucked at her sensitive skin, taunting her with catlike swipes of his tongue and careful teething. He gave her other breast equal attention a short while later.

She lost control suddenly, her insides shattering with a kind of violence that made her scream as she climaxed. Glittery sensations swept over her, so powerful that in the aftermath of her release she slumped across his chest, gasping for breath as she clung to him.

Thomas embraced her, his hands shaking as he stroked her back and hips. He shifted their bodies a short while later, tucking her beneath him. He moved slowly at first, teasing her with a shallow pumping motion, then deepening his penetration.

"Yes. Oh, yes," Geneva whispered as she twined her arms around his neck and brought his lips down to hers.

He maintained rigid control over himself, his body glistening with sweat as he rekindled her desire. She writhed beneath him, surrendering completely to the incendiary feelings flowing anew through her body. Circling his hips with her legs, she met his every thrust with a counterthrust. She slanted her lips across his and sucked his tongue into her mouth.

She felt complete as a result of his possession, felt a sense of recognition. She'd found the mate she had longed for during her years alone. As he plumbed her depths, she imprinted on her heart the taste and feel of his passion and sensuality.

Neither one held back in the minutes that followed. They teased. They tantalized. Their bodies blended with a fluidity that heightened their pleasure even more. The turbulence of their mating finally pushed them both over the edge.

Geneva cried out, her climax so thorough that her entire body went stiff. Her insides clenched repeatedly. Sensation after sensation rippled through her, over and over again until she felt disconnected from everything in the world but Thomas.

He succumbed to her tumultuous release and went spinning beyond control just moments later, his own need for completion too strong to resist any longer. His body spasmed, and he splintered apart. He moaned her name and his love for her.

Geneva, her face pressed against his neck, didn't realize that Thomas had spoken to her.

Sinking down over her soon after, Thomas struggled for air as he cradled Geneva against his chest and rolled them both onto their sides. He turned off the lamp. The warmth of the fire warded off the threat of a chill, so they simply held each other in the darkness.

Geneva waited until Thomas had fallen asleep before she eased out of his embrace and got up from the couch. She located her panties and bra, slipping into them as she stood before the fireplace. As she stared at the dwindling flames, she battled the urge to walk away from Thomas again.

No, she thought, the time for running had long since passed.

Geneva turned away from the fireplace, but she paused when she noticed that Thomas had awakened and was watching her. When he said nothing, she reached for her sweater and slipped it over her head. She hoped she might feel less vulnerable with her clothes on.

"Running away again, Geneva?" Still reclining on the couch, he made no effort to conceal his nakedness.

She glanced away, trying to quell her response to his powerful male body. Desire spilled like heated honey into her bloodstream, nonetheless.

"Nothing to say?" he pressed.

"You may not want to hear what I have to say."

"Shouldn't I be the one to make that decision?" he asked after shifting into a seated position on the couch.

"You're the only one who can, Thomas."

Geneva sank down onto the opposite end of the couch after pulling on her slacks. Her gaze drifted back to the fireplace as she tried to assemble her thoughts. A chill traveled through her, prompting her to draw her legs up and wrap her arms around them. Sighing softly, she finally looked at Thomas, but she didn't speak right away.

"I'm listening," he prompted after several moments of silence.

She nodded. "As you already know, I make it a rule never to discuss with anyone other than my family the life I led before I moved to Cedar Grove, but I'm going to break that rule this one time."

It occurred to her then that Thomas was no different from Nicholas Benteen or the others who made up his gypsy band of ex-warriors. Her family would respect a man like Thomas Coltrane, even welcome him into their ranks if he felt inclined to seek their acceptance and friendship.

Was she fantasizing? she wondered. She sensed that she was guilty of foolishness, but a moment of wishful dreaming offered a small measure of comfort at that particular moment.

Geneva consciously gathered up the threads of her courage and refocused on the task before her. "My father, as I told you, was a munitions specialist. He altered various types of weapons as a hobby. He also rigged and placed detonating devices in parts of the world where no sane man would venture, and he devised some of the most intricate bombs ever created. He did these things all over the globe for most of his adult life and for the highest bidders. He was a charming man, always filled with laughter and tall tales. He was happiest when he was smack in the middle of an armed insurrection or a backwater revolution. People are still using his designs, even though he's been dead for eighteen years. He was a legend in his own time, but he was a mercenary, pure and simple."

Geneva paused for a moment, then continued. "Political upheaval turned him on. Patrick was brilliant, but he was also reckless and quite amoral at times. His association with Nicholas settled him down, though, and placed him in the position of supporting causes that were, to a certain degree, morally defensible or backed by the U.S. government during the last fifteen years of his life. He admired Nicholas, even loved him like a son, so he abided by his rules. Fortunately for me, Nicholas was already a part of his life when I arrived on the scene, but I was still involved in the violence and destruction of their world."

Thomas interrupted. "Are you taking responsibility for your father's actions? Because if you are, you needn't. Just because Patrick had the poor judgment to drag you to hell and back as a teenager and a young adult doesn't mean that his sins are your burden to carry, Geneva. They never were. His penance is his own to pay, for God's sake!"

Her chin trembled, but Geneva smothered

the array of emotions rising up inside of her. "People died."

"That's what happens in wartime," he reminded her, his facial expression grim.

She pushed forward, determined to make all her points. Half the truth was like no truth at all, she knew from personal experience. "For the last twelve years, there's been a contract out on my life. I've had to be very careful. I haven't lived the way most people do. I doubt I even know how."

"I figured out that much that first day. Jamal, the Mossad, Nick encouraging you to stop worrying because the guy was neutralized." He shook his head in obvious amazement. "Hell of a word, by the way. It got my attention, and I drew the obvious conclusion."

Agonizing over what she still needed to tell him, Geneva lacked the strength at that moment to lift her hands. "I . . . am . . . my . . . father's . . . daughter," she enunciated with great care.

"But you aren't his conscience," Thomas protested. "You were an innocent witness."

She shot to her feet, unable to sit still any longer. "You don't understand! I have never been innocent. I am my father's daughter, Thomas," she said again, signing rapidly as she wandered around the sitting room. "In every possible way, and then some. I inherited his technical skills. I was as good, if not better,

than he was, and I took his place when he died
in Algiers on my nineteenth birthday. I was
not an observer or an innocent. I was a highly
skilled explosives expert, and I worked in that
capacity, primarily for the CIA, for several
years until a faulty piece of equipment malfunctioned, nearly killed me, and destroyed
my ability to hear. Without Nicholas and the
others, I would be dead.''

Thomas stared at her.

''There's something else you need to understand. I am not ashamed of who or what I
was, nor am I ashamed of the people who
cared for me before and after the accident, so
do not presume to judge me, my life, or my
friends. I know how different we are, and I
know that very few people are capable of accepting us. My only regret is that violence is
how the world solves its problems. I know
from very painful personal experience that
there are better ways.''

Geneva made herself wait then, her eyes
darting back and forth between the clock on
the far wall and the disbelief etched into his
hard-featured face.

Silence stretched tautly between them.

Two minutes passed.

Then a third.

Still, neither one of them spoke.

Only her pride kept Geneva from suc-
cumbing to the anguish she felt. Certain that

his continuing silence was rejection, she turned away from him, her shoulders sagging with defeat.

Geneva stepped into her knee boots. "Have a nice life, Thomas Coltrane," she said without looking at him again.

She walked out of the sitting room without another word. She felt so empty and cold inside that she knew she'd never be warm again.

Geneva hardly remembered getting into her car or driving out of Cedar Grove and along the back roads through the falling snow, but she arrived in one piece at Nicholas and Hannah's home an hour later. Only then did she let herself grieve for what might have been.

ELEVEN

Thomas recognized that he'd made an error in judgment the instant the door to his office slammed shut.

The sound jarred him beyond the paralysis of his disbelief. It also infused him with a sudden burst of energy. He surged up from the couch and reached for his clothes, furious with himself. In his struggle not to overreact to Geneva's remarks, he hadn't allowed himself to react at all.

He dressed hurriedly, then made his way into his office. He controlled his first impulse, which was to go after her and tell her that he didn't care about her past. In truth, he didn't. But the pragmatism and cold logic that invariably guided his instincts when he was threatened with failure told him that he needed a more complete picture of Geneva and what she faced in the future before he spoke to her.

Thomas loved her, but he knew in his heart that love wasn't always enough between a man and a woman. He had to be absolutely certain of his ability to protect her. If he couldn't keep her out of harm's way, then he would fail them both. That realization enabled him to contain some of the emotional turmoil he felt, despite the difficulty of the task.

His memory of her shattered facial expression stayed with him, though, haunting him as he picked up the telephone and dialed a local number.

Nicholas Benteen answered on the second ring.

"This is Tom Coltrane. We have to talk." He paused briefly. "Now. I'll need directions."

He fell silent, listening to Nicholas, who spoke in a terse, unemotional voice. He didn't bother to write down the directions once Benteen revealed that he lived high atop Eagle Ridge Summit, a spot Thomas had often frequented as a boy in search of adventure in the mountains surrounding Cedar Grove.

Shrugging into his coat and pocketing his keys, Thomas made his way downstairs to the parking lot behind the building and climbed into his car. As he drove through the darkness and the falling snow, he grappled with a variety of emotions. One in particular, one that he hadn't been forced to deal with in many years, emerged to dominate the others.

Fear.

His gut-wrenching fear that he'd already lost Geneva.

Gripping the steering wheel, Thomas promised himself that he would move heaven and earth before he allowed her to disappear from his life. No matter the cost, no matter the sacrifices required of him, she would be a part of his future. With or without Benteen's cooperation.

The two men faced off in the office that Nicholas kept in his home. Furnished with state-of-the-art security equipment more suitable for a war room in the depths of the Pentagon than the office of a successful author, it served to reinforce his concern for the jeopardy that Geneva had lived with since her early teens.

"You look like you could use a drink," Nicholas observed. "Help yourself." He gestured in the direction of the bar.

Thomas shook his head. "A drink is the last thing I want right now."

Nicholas sat down at his desk. He pressed a button on the console built into the desktop, then settled back in his chair, his expression speculative as he met his guest's gaze.

"What do you want?" Nicholas asked, the bluntness of his personality much in evidence.

"Facts." He sank into a chair that offered him an unobstructed view of Benteen.

Nicholas pondered Thomas for several silent minutes, then nodded.

In another wing of the house, Hannah Benteen closed the door to her daughter's room and made her way down the hallway. She paused in the open doorway of a small sitting room.

Geneva asked, "Is the baby all right?"

Smiling at the reference to her infant daughter, Hannah entered the room and sat down. She both signed and spoke her reply. "Asleep for now, but that will end as soon as she's hungry again." She studied Geneva for a moment, then asked, "Are you feeling any better?"

Geneva shrugged. "I think I'm all cried out for the moment. I'm just tired. I should go home and leave you all in peace."

"Stay, why don't you? Mom and Dad are spending a few days at Sean's place. We've missed your company."

"I'm not much company for anyone, I'm afraid."

"You're in love with him, aren't you?"

Tears flooded her eyes yet again. Geneva

blinked them back, but one slipped free and rolled down her cheek. Unable to speak, she nodded. The compassion in Hannah's face made her sigh. She envied the life Hannah and Nicholas shared, but she didn't begrudge them the happiness they'd found together. She just longed for the same sense of belonging for herself, a sense of belonging that she doubted she would ever experience firsthand.

"Thomas Coltrane is here," Hannah said.

Geneva paled. "I don't want to see him."

"He doesn't know you're here, so he hasn't asked for you."

She remembered then that she'd parked in the garage, rather than in front of the dwelling. Thomas wouldn't know of her presence at the Benteen's unless she made him aware of it, and she had no plans to do anything so unwise.

"He called a little while ago and told Nicholas that he wanted to speak with him privately."

Geneva shrugged, trying to appear indifferent. Wrapping her arms around her middle, she leaned back against the cushions of the couch and stared up at the ceiling.

She ached so badly inside that she wanted to wail, but she bit back her pain and kept herself under control. Thomas might be physically close by, she realized, but he was a million miles away in terms of their relationship.

What relationship? she asked herself. Their short-lived affair was over, and she needed to adjust to that fact.

Hannah straightened suddenly, her gaze flying to the intercom on the wall by the door.

Geneva felt rather than saw Hannah's sudden movement. "What's wrong?"

"Nicholas just turned on the intercom in his office. The sound of his voice startled me."

"He must have bumped the switch. You'd better let him know."

Hannah smiled, sinking back in her chair. "I've discovered that my husband is a very deliberate creature. If the intercom is on, it's because he wants it that way."

Geneva knew Nicholas too well not to figure out the method to his current madness. "Being deaf has an up side," she remarked bitterly, glad that she wouldn't be able to hear a conversation between Thomas and Nicholas.

"For heaven's sake, Geneva, quit punishing yourself."

Startled by Hannah's vehement expression, she insisted she was not.

"Then don't act like a martyr. You shocked the man, you gave him two or three minutes to react to a reality you've had years to come to terms with, and then you marched out the door."

"He's history, Hannah. I don't want him."

"This is foolish."

"No, this is survival. My survival."

"You're not even curious why he's here?" Hannah pressed her.

Not bothering to answer, Geneva got to her feet and paced the sitting room. She *was* curious, but in spite of her desire to know what the two men were saying, she refused to admit the truth to Hannah.

"We both know you are," Hannah remarked when Geneva glanced at her. "I'll try to keep up with both of them."

Geneva stumbled to an abrupt stop as Hannah began to sign. She failed to find the strength within herself to turn away. Instead, she kept her gaze on Hannah's swiftly moving hands.

Hannah Cassidy Benteen signed and finger-spelled with a deftness that spoke of her years as a teacher and an advocate for abused and handicapped children.

"Are there any more out there like Jamal who want her dead?" Thomas asked only seconds before Hannah signed the question.

"She told you about Jamal?" Nicholas asked in reply.

"Not specifically, but I overheard a good portion of a conversation between the two of you one day. I put the pieces together after the fact. Geneva simply confirmed my conclusions."

"What else have you done?"

"I called a friend at Langley yesterday."

"How much do you know about us?"

"Not much. Your privacy is intact. It will remain that way. I'm not inclined to dig any deeper unless the need arises."

"How much?" Nicholas demanded.

Hannah smiled at her husband's persistence, a character trait that she often said made her crazy.

"Damn little, aside from the fact that most of you were mercenaries, available for hire by anybody financially solvent. You were also periodic employees of the CIA. Geneva admitted that she did covert work for the CIA for several years."

"She didn't work for anyone but the agency, Coltrane. Not ever. I made sure of it."

"For her sake, I'm relieved. It may sound like I'm splitting hairs, but there's a major difference between an operative and a mercenary. That distinction is important for Geneva's peace of mind."

Geneva and Hannah looked at each other when the two men paused in their conversation. Geneva's heart raced. Although she couldn't actually hear his voice, it was clear to her that Thomas was genuinely concerned about her. His words weren't at all judgmental, which also surprised her. She'd expected outright condemnation. Still, she couldn't forget the distaste she'd seen in his eyes just a few short hours ago.

Hannah began to sign again.

Geneva paid close attention.

"You know exactly what she did, don't you?"

"She filled me in on some of the facts."

"I have the impression that the conversation didn't go well."

"You've spoken to her?"

"Yes."

"She was upset. You didn't answer my question, by the way. Is she in jeopardy even with Jamal out of the game?"

"It's doubtful, but not totally out of the question. Most of the threats have been neutralized. Geneva has been away from the business for a lot of years. Living reclusively is more of a habit for her than anything else."

"Revenge rarely has a time limit, Nick."

"A reasonable amount of concern is justified. Paranoia is not."

"I can protect her, but only if I know what she's up against."

"You rejected her, Tom. It's doubtful she'll give you another opportunity to do it again."

"I didn't reject her."

"Then what would you call what you did?"

"In a nutshell, I didn't react one way or another. I was shocked."

"Most people are, which is why the family remains apart from most of the world."

"Hell of a way to live."

"It's lonely, especially for a woman like Geneva. That's why I encouraged her to start a business. She needed to create a new identity, and she needed time to make peace with the past. Thanks to some friends who are still in the business, I've been able to track Jamal. I've known for a while that his days were numbered. My contacts also tell me that Geneva's name has disappeared from the more dangerous hit lists. The only issue that remains is the possibility of kidnapping for the purpose of forcing her to create explosive devices, but there are too many other qualified people willing to do the job. I'm convinced that she's finally in the clear."

"She's a remarkable woman."

"Her friends know that. I had the idea that you did, too, but you've made me doubt my judgment about you."

"Tell me about Patrick."

The two women glanced at each other once more. They both knew that Nicholas had no tolerance for anyone who criticized his deceased comrade-in-arms. The bond between Nicholas and Patrick in particular had run very deep.

"Patrick was her father, and he loved her."

"You don't mind if I have a hard time believing that."

"I don't care what you believe, Coltrane. I knew Patrick Talmadge. He wasn't mean-spirited, although he was self-indulgent at times. He never should have involved Geneva in his world, but he did. She's dealt with the results of the choices her father made with strength and courage. The past can't be changed. Geneva knows that and she's accepted it. I suspect you've learned the same lesson, although for very different reasons."

"You checked me out, didn't you?"

"Of course. She's far too important to all of us to be placed at risk."

"Do your enemies know where you are?"

"The few who are still alive probably do, but they know that they expose themselves to a greater danger if they come after me. Bottom line: the odds are against them."

"How do I protect her?"

"Why would you want to, especially now that you know the truth about her?"

"It doesn't matter why."

"Do you have more questions about her past?"

"If I do, I'll ask Geneva. For the record, my only real concern is her safety. I don't want anything to happen to her, so I expect to be kept up to speed if threats of any kind emerge."

"Sounds like you're planning on hanging around, which might be tough since she doesn't want you within a hundred miles of her right now. How do you intend to handle the situation?"

"I'll handle it."

"What are your feelings for her?"

"That isn't any of your concern."

Hannah suddenly grinned.

"What?" signed Geneva.

"Nicholas is laughing."

Startled, Geneva asked, "Why?"

Instead of answering, Hannah asked, "Men are so obvious, don't you think?"

Exasperated with what she viewed as her own cowardice, Geneva suddenly said, "I'm going to speak with Thomas. Nicholas doesn't belong in the middle of this mess."

"I wish you would. Thomas is obviously worried about you."

"I can take care of myself," Geneva retorted.

"But do you want to have to all of the time?"

She sighed, a little deflated by the question. "Not really."

Hannah urged, "The man loves you, Geneva, and you obviously love him, so let your heart guide you, not your pride."

With Hannah's advice echoing in her head, Geneva left the sitting room and hurried down the hallway. It didn't take her long to reach the office in an adjacent wing of the house.

Nicholas opened the door just as she raised her hand to knock. "Take as much time as you need," he signed before he strolled out of the room and pulled the door shut behind him.

Geneva paused after taking several steps into the office. "Why are you here?" she asked. The uncertainty she felt reverberated within her heart and soul, but she refused to make a fool of herself by revealing her unsettled emotions.

"There were some things I needed to understand before I came after you."

"And do you? Understand, I mean."

He nodded. "I think so, but I'm still concerned about your safety."

She stiffened her spine. "I don't want or need a bodyguard."

"Well, you've got one, dammit, so get used to the idea."

"No!" she exclaimed, not bothering to sign the word.

"Marry me."

She stared at him, shocked by his proposal. "That can't and won't happen," she insisted, although it killed her to deny the one thing she wanted most in the world with this man.

"Why?"

"We're too different."

"Because I can hear, and you can't?"

"Because what I was in the past will eventually come back to haunt us both. I have no intention of having the ax fall on you."

"I know who you are now, Geneva. That's all that matters to me."

"You'd be compromising your standards."

"Standards are pretty useless if they keep us apart. Besides, I'm no Boy Scout. I never was, and I never will be."

"But we are apart. Worlds apart."

He took a step forward. "You're wrong. You couldn't be more wrong."

She backed up. "I saw your reaction to what I told you. You were appalled, Thomas, as any rational person would be."

"I was shocked. I was also reacting to the fact that you've experienced so much pain, especially since you didn't have to in the first place."

"But I did. Part of what I am is based on what I was."

"Flimsy reasoning. I'm sure you can do better if you put your mind to it."

"Damn you!"

"I think I will be if you shut me out of your life."

She blinked in surprise at his admission. No one had ever said such a thing to her.

He moved forward yet again.

She knew the closed door was behind her, so she held her ground.

Thomas paused in front of her, but he didn't touch her.

Geneva held her breath, wanting to feel his hands on her body, but also fearful that he might actually fulfill that need. She would be lost if he touched her. Utterly and completely lost. She wondered if he knew the extent of his power where she was concerned. Something in his gaze told her he did, but that he wouldn't ever abuse it.

"I know the price that comes with hurting another human being, Geneva. That's why I left my practice in San Diego, and I'm learning to live with my past."

She looked up at him, wanting to believe that he meant what he said. Doubt, however, made her ask, "How do you know you won't change your mind later? How can you be so sure that you won't feel compelled to judge me?"

"God is your judge, Geneva. Not me. Never me. Not in a million years. I've got my own ghosts, not to mention more regrets than I know what to do with." He shook his head, his expression troubled. "I thought you trusted me."

"I did," she whispered.

"And you don't now?"

"I . . ." A tide of longing suddenly

washed over her, and she knew then that she couldn't lie to him. "I do trust you, Thomas."

"Then trust me enough to believe me when I tell you that I'm in love with you."

Stunned, she stared at him.

"You have a choice to make. A life sentence in a prison of your own design, or a life with me, the man who loves you."

Thomas reached out for her and gathered her into his arms. He held her for several silent minutes.

Geneva savored the gentleness of his embrace. She shuddered, her fingers digging into his lower back as she held on to him. The thought of never touching him or being touched by him again, of not sharing their love and their lives, made her feel so empty inside.

He released her when she shifted to free herself.

"I don't want to harm your reputation," she said.

"You couldn't. I want you in my life," he countered.

The temptation to fling caution to the wind surfaced within her. "I want to believe it's possible. But I'm also trying to be realistic," she insisted, her love for him prompting her to try to protect him from making a mistake.

His expression determined, he said, "My

reality is very simple. I love you. I want you to be my wife. I want children and a real home. I want to wake up every morning for the rest of my life and find you next to me. I just want to love you. And I will protect you with my life if anyone tries to harm you."

Tears brimmed in her eyes. He'd voiced every one of her fantasies. She already knew he was the consummate lover, and now she realized he was so much more. He was the man who loved her unconditionally.

"You're what I want, Geneva," Thomas continued. "I've waited my entire life for you, but the decision rests in your hands now. Either you choose to believe in and trust what we feel for each other, or you throw it all away. It all boils down to a choice. Your choice."

She gazed up at him, amazed by his willingness to risk everything. And he was asking her to do the same, she realized. She exhaled shakily, aware now that Thomas was right. Just like love and commitment, belief and faith and trust were choices. She knew then that only cowardice on her part would keep them apart.

"Love me enough to share the future with me," he said encouragingly.

"I do love you, Thomas, more than I ever thought myself capable of loving a man."

He reached out, his fingers trembling as he

traced the curve of her cheek. A muscle ticked in his hard cheek, but he didn't rush her, didn't push her. He simply waited.

Geneva turned her head, her lips whispering across his fingertips. Her eyes fell closed for a long moment. She felt his strength in his touch and in his patience. She knew him well enough to realize that there would never be boundaries or restrictions on the kind of love he offered. Thomas Coltrane did nothing halfway. His commitment to her would be permanent and all-encompassing and based on his love for her.

This was the kind of love she'd longed for her entire life. He was the kind of man she'd prayed for, and she didn't possess the strength or stubbornness to deny herself the realization of her dreams any longer.

Geneva smiled up at him. For the first time in many years, she suddenly didn't feel compelled to guard her heart and protect her emotions.

"Will you marry me, Geneva?"

Not able to deprive either one of them the happiness they both sought, she finger-spelled her reply, "Yes, Thomas, I'll marry you."

"Why?" he asked.

"Because I love you and because I trust you with my heart and my life."

"That was the right answer, Ms. Talmadge."

Geneva grinned. "I certainly hope so."

Thomas seized her, drew her into his arms, and swung her around.

"You're going to make me dizzy," she exclaimed, her blue eyes sparkling with laughter.

Thomas smiled as he lowered her to the floor. "I know a lot of ways to make you dizzy."

She tapped his chest and cautioned, "Don't brag."

"That was a promise."

"Maybe you'd better give me a sample. That way I can be absolutely certain that you're good husband material."

He accepted her challenge.

Geneva welcomed his lips when Thomas claimed her mouth in a searching, intoxicating kiss that left her breathless and clinging to his broad shoulders when it finally ended several minutes later.

"Now do you believe me?" he asked.

"Always." She moved back into his embrace, circled his neck with her arms, and tugged his lips down to hers for yet another sample of his passion—a passion that she knew would last a lifetime.

THE EDITORS' CORNER

Fall is just around the corner, but there's one way you can avoid the chill in the air. Cuddle up with the LOVESWEPT novels coming your way next month. These heart-melting tales of romance are guaranteed to keep you warm with the heat of passion.

Longtime LOVESWEPT favorite Peggy Webb returns with a richly emotional tale of forbidden desire in **INDISCREET**, LOVESWEPT #802. Bolton Gray Wolf appears every inch a savage when he arrives to interview Virginia Haven, but the moment she rides up on a white Arabian stallion, challenge glittering in her eyes, he knows he will make her his! Even as his gaze leaves her breathless, Virginia vows he'll never tame her; but once they touch, she has no choice but to surrender. Peggy Webb offers a spectacular glimpse into the astonishing mysteries of love in a tale of fiery magic and unexpected miracles.

Marcia Evanick delivers her award-winning blend of love and laughter in **SECOND-TIME LUCKY**, LOVESWEPT #803. Luke Callahan arrives without warning to claim a place in Dayna's life, but he reminds her too much of the heartbreak she'd endured during her marriage to his brother! Luke wants to help raise her sons, but even more, he wants the woman he's secretly loved for years. Dared by his touch, drawn by his warmth to open her heart, Dayna feels her secret hopes grow strong. In a novel that explores the soul-deep hunger of longing and loneliness, Marcia Evanick weaves a wonderful tapestry of emotion and humor, dark secrets and tender joys.

A love too long denied finds a second chance in **DESTINY STRIKES TWICE**, LOVESWEPT #804, by Maris Soule. Effie Sanders returns to the lake to pack up her grandmother's house and the memory of summers spent tagging along with her sister Bernadette . . . and Parker Morgan. With his blue eyes and lean, tanned muscles, Parker had always been out of Effie's reach, had never noticed her in the shadow of her glamorous sister. Never—until an older, overworked Parker comes to his family's cottage to learn to relax and finds the irrepressible girl he once knew has grown up to become a curvy, alluring woman. And suddenly he is anything but relaxed. Maris Soule has created a story that ignites with fiery desire and ripples with tender emotion.

And finally, Faye Hughes gives the green light to scandal in **LICENSED TO SIN**, LOVESWEPT #805. In a voice so sensual it makes her toes curl, Nick Valdez invites Jane Steele to confess her secrets, making her fear that her cover has been blown! But she knows she's safe when the handsome gambler then suggests they join forces to investigate rigged games at a riverboat casino. She agrees to his scheme, knowing that sharing close quarters with Nick will be risky temptation. In this blend of steamy romance and fast-paced adventure, Faye Hughes reveals the tantalizing pleasures of playing dangerous games and betting it all on the roll of the dice.

Happy reading!

With warmest wishes,

Beth de Guzman   Shauna Summers
Senior Editor   Editor

P.S. Watch for these Bantam women's fiction titles coming in September. With her mesmerizing voice and spellbinding touch of contemporary romantic suspense, Kay Hooper wowed readers and reviewers alike with her Bantam hardcover debut, **AMANDA**—and it's soon coming your way in paperback. Nationally bestselling author Patricia Potter shows her flair for humor and warm emotion in **THE MARSHAL AND THE HEIRESS**; this one has a western lawman lassoing the bad guys all the way in Scotland! From Adrienne deWolfe, the author *Ro-*

mantic Times hailed as "an exciting new talent," comes **TEXAS LOVER,** the enthralling tale of a Texas Ranger, a beautiful Yankee woman, and a houseful of orphans. Be sure to see next month's LOVESWEPTs for a preview of these exceptional novels. And immediately following this page, preview the Bantam women's fiction titles on sale *now*!

Don't miss these extraordinary books
by your favorite Bantam authors

On sale in July:
PRINCE OF SHADOWS
by Susan Krinard

WALKING RAIN
by Susan Wade

No one could tame him. Except a woman
in love.

From the electrifying talent of
Susan Krinard
author of *Star-Crossed* and *Prince of Wolves*
comes a breathtaking, magical new
romance
PRINCE OF SHADOWS

"Susan Krinard has set the standard for
today's fantasy romance."—*Affaire de Coeur*

*Scarred by a tragic accident, Alexandra Warrington has
come back to the Minnesota woods looking for refuge and a
chance to carry on her passionate study of wolves. But her
peace is shattered when she awakes one morning to find a
total stranger in her bed. Magnificently muscled and perfectly naked, he exudes a wildness that frightens her and a
haunting fear that touches her. Yet Alex doesn't realize
that this handsome savage is a creature out of myth, a wolf
transformed into a man. And when the town condemns
him for a terrible crime, all she knows is that she is dan-
gerously close to loving him and perilously committed to
saving him . . . no matter what the cost.*

The wolf was on his feet again, standing by the door.
She forgot her resolve not to stare. Magnificent was
the only word for him, even as shaky as he was. He

lifted one paw and scraped it against the door, turning to look at her in a way that couldn't be misunderstood.

He wanted out. Alex felt a sudden, inexplicable panic. He wasn't ready. Only moments before she'd been debating what to do with him, and now her decision was being forced.

Once she opened that door he'd be gone, obeying instincts older and more powerful than the ephemeral trust he'd given her on the edge of death. In his weakened state, once back in the woods he'd search out the easiest prey he could find.

Livestock. Man's possessions, lethally guarded by guns and poison.

Alex backed away, toward the hall closet, where she kept her seldom-used dart gun. In Canada she and her fellow researchers had used guns like it to capture wolves for collaring and transfer to new homes in the northern United States. She hadn't expected to need it here.

Now she didn't have any choice. Shadow leaned against the wall patiently as she retrieved the gun and loaded it out of his sight. She tucked it into the loose waistband of her jeans, at the small of her back, and started toward the door.

Shadow wagged his tail. Only once, and slowly, but the simple gesture cut her to the heart. It was as if he saw her as another wolf. As if he recognized what she'd tried to do for him. She edged to the opposite side of the door and opened it.

Biting air swirled into the warmth of the cabin. Shadow stepped out, lifting his muzzle to the sky, breathing in a thousand subtle scents Alex couldn't begin to imagine.

She followed him and sat at the edge of the porch

as he walked stiffly into the clearing. "What are you?" she murmured. "Were you captive once? Were you cut off from your own kind?"

He heard her, pausing in his business and pricking his ears. Golden eyes held answers she couldn't interpret with mere human senses.

"I know what you aren't, Shadow. You aren't meant to be anyone's pet. Or something to be kept in a cage and stared at. I wish to God I could let you go."

The wolf whuffed softly. He looked toward the forest, and Alex stiffened, reaching for the dart gun. But he turned back and came to her again, lifted his paw and set it very deliberately on her knee.

Needing her. Trusting her. Accepting. His huge paw felt warm and familiar, like a friend's touch.

Once she'd loved being touched. By her mother, by her grandparents—by Peter. She'd fought so hard to get over that need, that weakness.

Alex raised her hand and felt it tremble. She let her fingers brush the wolf's thick ruff, stroke down along his massive shoulder. Shadow sighed and closed his eyes to slits of contentment.

Oh, God. In a minute she'd be flinging her arms around his great shaggy neck. *Wrong, wrong.* He was a wolf, not a pet dog. She withdrew her hands and clasped them in her lap.

He nudged her hand. His eyes, amber and intelligent, regarded her without deception. Like no human eyes in the world.

"I won't let them kill you, Shadow," she said hoarsely. "No matter what you are, or what happens. I'll help you. I promise." She closed her eyes. "I've made promises I wasn't able to keep, but not this time. Not this time."

Promises. One to a strange, lost boy weeping over the bodies of two murdered wolves. A boy who, like the first Shadow, she'd never found again.

And another promise to her mother, who had died to save her.

The ghost of one had returned to her at last.

The wolf whined and patted her knee, his claws snagging on her jeans. A gentle snow began to fall, thick wet flakes that kissed Alex's cheeks with the sweetness of a lover. She turned her face up to the sky's caress. Shadow leaned against her heavily, his black pelt dusted with snowflakes.

If only I could go back, she thought. Back to the time when happiness had been such a simple thing, when a wolf could be a friend and fairy tales were real. She sank her fingers deeper into Shadow's fur.

If only—you were human. A man as loyal, as protective, as fundamentally honest as a wolf with its own. A man who could never exist in the real world. A fairy-tale hero, a prince ensorcelled.

She allowed herself a bitter smile. The exact opposite of Peter, in fact.

And you think you'd deserve such a man, if he did exist?

She killed that line of thought before it could take hold, forcing her fingers to unclench from Shadow's fur. "What am I going to do, Shadow?" she said.

The wolf set his forepaws on the porch and heaved his body up, struggling to lift himself to the low platform. Alex watched his efforts with a last grasp at objectivity.

Now. Dart him now, and there will still be time to contact the ADC. She clawed at the dart gun and pulled it from her waistband.

But Shadow looked up at her in that precise moment, and she was lost. "I can't," she whispered. She let her arm go slack. The dart gun fell from her nerveless fingers, landing in the snow. She stared at it blindly.

Teeth that could rend and tear so efficiently closed with utmost gentleness around her empty hand. Shadow tugged until she had no choice but to look at him again.

She knew what he wanted. She hesitated only a moment before opening the door. Shadow padded into the cabin and found the place she had made for him by the stove, stretching out full-length on the old braided rug, chin on paws.

"You've made it easy for me, haven't you?" she asked him, closing the door behind her. "You're trapped, and I can keep you here until . . . until I can figure out what to do with you."

The wolf gazed at her so steadily that she was almost certain that he'd known exactly what he was doing. She wanted to go to him and huddle close, feel the warmth of his great body and the sumptuous texture of his fur. But she had risked too much already. In the morning she'd have to reach a decision about him, and she knew how this would end—how it must end—sooner or later.

Shadow would be gone, and she'd be alone.

Feeling decades older than her twenty-seven years, Alex took her journal from the kitchen and retreated into the darkness of her bedroom. She paused at the door, her hand on the knob, and closed it with firm and deliberate pressure.

She stripped off her clothes and hung them neatly in the tiny closet, retrieving a clean pair of long underwear. The journal lay open on the old wooden bed table, waiting for the night's final entry.

It's ironic, Mother. I thought I'd become strong. Objective. I can't even succeed in this.

Her flannel bedsheets were cold; she drew the blankets up high around her chin, an old childhood habit she'd never shaken. Once it had made her feel safe, as if her mother's own hands had tucked her in. Now it only made her remember how false a comfort it truly was.

It was a long time before she slept. The sun was streaming through the curtains when she woke again. She lay very still, cherishing the ephemeral happiness that came to her at the very edge of waking.

She wasn't alone. There was warmth behind her on the bed, a familiar weight at her back that pulled down the mattress. The pressure of another body, masculine and solid.

Peter. She kept her eyes closed. It wasn't often that Peter slept the night through and was still beside her when she woke. And when he was . . .

His hand brushed her hip, hot through the knit fabric of her long underwear. When Peter was with her in the morning, it was because he wanted to make love. She gasped silently as his palm moved down to the upper edge of her thigh and then back up again, drawing the hem of her top up and up until he found skin.

Alex shuddered. It had been so long. Her belly tightened in anticipation. Peter wanted her. He *wanted* her. His fingers stroked along her ribs with delicate tenderness. They brushed the lower edge of her breast. Her nipples hardened almost painfully.

The arousal was a release, running hot in her blood. In a moment she would roll over and into his arms. In a moment she'd give herself up to the sex, to the searing intensity of physical closeness, seizing it for as long as it lasted.

But for now Peter was caressing her gently, without his usual impatience—taking time to make her ready, to feed her excitement—and she savored it. She wouldn't ruin the moment with words. Peter wasn't usually so silent. He liked talking before and after making love. About his plans, his ambitions. Their future.

All she could hear of him now was his breathing, sonorous and steady. His palm rested at the curve of her waist, the fingers making small circles on her skin.

His fingers. Callused fingers. She could feel their slight roughness. Blunt at the tips, not tapered. Big hands.

Big hands. Too big.

Wrongness washed through her in a wave of adrenaline. She snapped open her eyes and stared at the cracked face of the old-fashioned alarm clock beside the bed. Granddad's alarm clock. And beyond, the wood plank walls of the cabin.

Not the apartment. Her cabin. Not the king-size bed but her slightly sprung double.

The hand at her waist stilled.

Alex jerked her legs and found them trapped under an implacable weight. A guttural, groaning sigh sounded in her ear.

Very slowly she turned her head.

A man lay beside her, sprawled across the bed with one leg pinning the blankets over hers. A perfectly naked, magnificently muscled stranger. His body was curled toward her, head resting on one arm. His other hand was on her skin. Straight, thick black hair shadowed his face.

Alex did no more than tense her body, but that was enough. The man moved; the muscles of his torso and flat belly rippled as he stretched and lifted his head. Yellow eyes met her gaze through the veil of his hair.

Yellow eyes. Clear as sunlight, fathomless as ancient amber. Eyes that almost stopped her heart.

For an instant—one wayward, crazy instant—Alex *knew* him. And then that bizarre sensation passed to be replaced with far more pragmatic instincts. She twisted and bucked to free her legs and shoved him violently, knocking his hand from her body. His eyes widened as he rocked backward on the narrow bed, clawed at the sheets and rolled over the far edge.

Alex tore the covers away and leaped from the bed, remembering belatedly that she'd left the dart gun outside, and Granddad's old rifle was firmly locked away in the hall closet. She spun for the door just as the man scrambled to his feet, tossing the hair from his eyes. Her hand had barely touched the doorknob when he lunged across the bed and grabbed her wrist in an iron grip.

Treacherous terror surged in her. She lashed out, and he caught her other hand. She stared at the man with his strange, piercing eyes and remembered she was not truly alone.

A wolf slept just beyond her door. A wolf that had trusted and accepted her as if she were a member of his pack. One of his own kind. A wolf that seemed to recognize the name she had given him.

"Shadow," she cried. It came out as a whisper. "Shadow!"

The man twitched. The muscles of his strong jaw stood out in sharp relief beneath tanned skin, and his fingers loosened around her wrists for one vital instant.

Alex didn't think. She ripped her arms free of his grasp, clasped her hands into a single fist, and struck him with all her strength.

Haunting, compelling, and richly atmospheric, this dazzling novel of romantic suspense marks the impressive debut of a talented new author.

WALKING RAIN

by Susan Wade

Eight years with a new name and a new identity had not succeeded in wiping out the horrors of the past. It was time for Amelia Rawlins to go home. Home to the New Mexico ranch where she had spent her childhood summers. Home to the place where she could feel her grandfather's spirit and carry on the work he had loved. But someone knew that Amelia had come back—Amelia, who should have died on that long-ago day . . . who should have known better than to think she could come back and start over with nothing more than a potter's wheel, a handful of wildflower seeds, and a stubborn streak. And someone was out to see that Amelia paid in full for her crimes. . . .

She drove up U.S. 54 from Interstate 10 because that was the way she had always come to the ranch. Her old pickup had held up well on the long drive from the East Coast, but now it rattled and jounced along the battered road. Amelia checked the rearview mirror often, making certain her potter's wheel was still securely lashed to the bed of the truck. It was her habit to watch her back.

She'd reached El Paso late in the afternoon and

stopped there to put gas in the truck. Between that stop and all the Juarez traffic, it was getting on toward evening by the time she left the city and, with it, the interstate. Now the mountains of the Tularosa basin rose on either side of the two-lane road: the soaring ridge of the Guadalupes to her east and the Organ Mountains, drier, more distant, to her west. The eastern range was heavily snowed, peaks gleaming pink in the fading light, and the evening sky was winter-brilliant. Narrow bands of clouds glowed like flamingo feathers above the Organs.

She had forgotten the crystalline stillness of the air here, forgotten the sunny chill of a New Mexico winter. How had that happened? Maybe that was the price she'd paid for forgetting the things she had to forget. Part of the price.

The sun flamed on the horizon, looking as if it would flow down the mountains to melt the world, and then it sank. Its light faded quickly from the sky; already the stars were taking their turn at ruling the deep blue reaches. Amelia rolled down her window, even though the temperature outside was plunging toward freezing. The desert smelled pungent and strong, and there was a hint of pine and piñon on the wind.

It was the wind that whipped tears to her eyes. Certainly the wind; she was not a woman who wept. But she was suddenly swept by a brilliant ache of homesickness—here, now, when she was very near the only home left to her—it caught at her violently. So violently that she almost turned the truck around and went away again.

To need something so much frightened her.

But she was tired, and she had only decided to come here when she could no longer face starting over somewhere new. She'd been rootless for too long.

So the truck spun on, winding north in the star-studded darkness, past the ghostly dunes of White Sands, north and then eventually east, to a narrower road, one that ran deep into the wrinkled land at the foot of the Guadalupes.

She made her way to the Crossroads by feel, and turned left without thinking. It was unsettling to be in a place so instantly familiar. The stars had come full out; the desert was bright beneath them. An ancient seabed, the Tularosa basin was now four thousand feet above sea level, and the air was thin, rarefied, so the starlight streamed through it undiminished. Amelia could see the beacon of the observatory to the south, high on the mountain, gleaming like a fallen star itself.

And then she was there, bumping the truck off the road next to the dirt lane that led to the house. The gate was closed. A new gate, one of those metal-barred affairs. Amelia left the truck idling when she got out, not sure it would start again if she turned it off after such a long run. But when she tried to open the gate, she found it padlocked. Her grandfather never did that.

She climbed up on the gate and looked toward the ranch house, sprawling among the cottonwood trees beyond the fields. No lights. No smoke from the chimney pipe. The windows were dark vacant blanks against the pale adobe walls of the house. She could see the looming windmill, its blades turning slowly in silhouette, but nothing else moved.

So maybe the ranch hadn't been leased to some-one else. Maybe her uncle hadn't decided she was dead and sold the place off. Maybe none of the things she'd been afraid of had happened.

She should have been relieved. But the homesickness was back, wilder than ever, and she realized that some part of her had expected her grandfather to be there waiting for her.

He was dead. Bound to be. He'd been seventy-six the last time she and her kid brother had come for the summer, and that was more than a dozen years ago. But one thing she had no doubt about—that Gramps had kept his word and left the property to her. She knew he had, as surely as she knew the pattern the cottonwoods' shadow would paint on the house in summer. This place was part of her.

She went back and cut off the truck. The silence was a living one, even in February. The rustle of a mouse in its nest and the faraway cry of a hunting night bird gathered on the wind. Amelia shivered. She put on her down vest, then took her backpack and her cooler out of the truck. Nobody would bother her things, not out here. Gramps used to say they could go a week without seeing another soul on this road.

He'd been exaggerating, of course. Something he was prone to. Amelia dropped the cooler over the fence, then swung herself over the gate. She picked up the cooler and started down the lane toward the house. The smell of the desert seemed even more sharply familiar now, thick with memories. She remembered racing Michael down this road on bikes—Gramps taking the two of them to collect native grasses by the old railroad tracks, Gramma baking biscuits in the cool of the morning. So many memories. A cascade of them.

They were falling around her like rain. Amelia bowed her head and walked up the road into it.

On sale in August:

AMANDA
by Kay Hooper

THE MARSHAL AND THE HEIRESS
by Patricia Potter

TEXAS LOVER
by Adrienne deWolfe

To enter the sweepstakes outlined below, you must respond by the date specified and follow all entry instructions published elsewhere in this offer.

DREAM COME TRUE SWEEPSTAKES

Sweepstakes begins 9/1/94, ends 1/15/96. To qualify for the Early Bird Prize, entry must be received by the date specified elsewhere in this offer. Winners will be selected in random drawings on 2/29/96 by an independent judging organization whose decisions are final. Early Bird winner will be selected in a separate drawing from among all qualifying entries.

Odds of winning determined by total number of entries received. Distribution not to exceed 300 million.

Estimated maximum retail value of prizes: Grand (1) $25,000 (cash alternative $20,000); First (1) $2,000; Second (1) $750; Third (50) $75; Fourth (1,000) $50; Early Bird (1) $5,000. Total prize value: $86,500.

Automobile and travel trailer must be picked up at a local dealer; all other merchandise prizes will be shipped to winners. Awarding of any prize to a minor will require written permission of parent/guardian. If a trip prize is won by a minor, s/he must be accompanied by parent/legal guardian. Trip prizes subject to availability and must be completed within 12 months of date awarded. Blackout dates may apply. Early Bird trip is on a space available basis and does not include port charges, gratuities, optional shore excursions and onboard personal purchases. Prizes are not transferable or redeemable for cash except as specified. No substitution for prizes except as necessary due to unavailability. Travel trailer and/or automobile license and registration fees are winners' responsibility as are any other incidental expenses not specified herein.

Early Bird Prize may not be offered in some presentations of this sweepstakes. Grand through third prize winners will have the option of selecting any prize offered at level won. All prizes will be awarded. Drawing will be held at 204 Center Square Road, Bridgeport, NJ 08014. Winners need not be present. For winners list (available in June, 1996), send a self-addressed, stamped envelope by 1/15/96 to: Dream Come True Winners, P.O. Box 572, Gibbstown, NJ 08027.

THE FOLLOWING APPLIES TO THE SWEEPSTAKES ABOVE:

No purchase necessary. No photocopied or mechanically reproduced entries will be accepted. Not responsible for lost, late, misdirected, damaged, incomplete, illegible, or postage-die mail. Entries become the property of sponsors and will not be returned.

Winner(s) will be notified by mail. Winner(s) may be required to sign and return an affidavit of eligibility/release within 14 days of date on notification or an alternate may be selected. Except where prohibited by law, entry constitutes permission to use of winners' names, hometowns, and likenesses for publicity without additional compensation. Void where prohibited or restricted. All federal, state, provincial, and local laws and regulations apply.

All prize values are in U.S. currency. Presentation of prizes may vary; values at a given prize level will be approximately the same. All taxes are winners' responsibility.

Canadian residents, in order to win, must first correctly answer a time-limited skill testing question administered by mail. Any litigation regarding the conduct and awarding of a prize in this publicity contest by a resident of the province of Quebec may be submitted to the Regie des loteries et courses du Quebec.

Sweepstakes is open to legal residents of the U.S., Canada, and Europe (in those areas where made available) who have received this offer.

Sweepstakes in sponsored by Ventura Associates, 1211 Avenue of the Americas, New York, NY 10036 and presented by independent businesses. Employees of these, their advertising agencies and promotional companies involved in this promotion, and their immediate families, agents, successors, and assignees shall be ineligible to participate in the promotion and shall not be eligible for any prizes covered herein.   SWP 3/95

DON'T MISS THESE FABULOUS
BANTAM WOMEN'S FICTION TITLES

On Sale in July

From the electrifying talent of
SUSAN KRINARD
leader in fantasy romance

PRINCE OF SHADOWS

Beautiful, dedicated wolf researcher Alexandra Warrington agonizes over the plight of a gorgeous wolf she discovers in the wild . . . until it vanishes, leaving a darkly handsome stranger in its place.

_____ 56777-2 $5.99/$7.99 in Canada

WALKING RAIN

by the highly acclaimed SUSAN WADE

This impressive debut novel is the haunting, romantic, and richly atmospheric story of a woman on an isolated New Mexico ranch being stalked by unseen forces. _____ 56865-5 $5.50/$6.99 in Canada